A HISTORY OF MONEY

A HISTORY OF MONEY

A Novel

ALAN PAULS

Translated from the Spanish by Ellie Robins

MELVILLE HOUSE
BROOKLYN • LONDON

A HISTORY OF MONEY

Originally published by Editorial Anagrama S. A.
as *Historia del dinero*
Copyright © 2013 by Alan Pauls
Translation copyright © 2015 by Ellie Robins

First Melville House printing: June 2015

Melville House Publishing   8 Blackstock Mews
          46 John Street   and   Islington
     Brooklyn, NY 11201   London N4 2BT

mhpbooks.com   facebook.com/mhpbooks   @melvillehouse

          Library of Congress Cataloging-in-Publication Data
Pauls, Alan.
   [Historia del dinero. English]
   A history of money : a novel / Alan Pauls ; translated by
   Ellie Robins.
      pages   cm
   ISBN 978-1-61219-423-3 (hardback)
   ISBN 978-1-61219-424-0 (ebook)
   1. Money—Fiction.   2. Argentina—Fiction.   I. Robins, Ellie,
translator.   II. Title.

PQ7798.26.A87H5713 2013
863'.64—dc23

                                        2014040204

          Design by Christopher King

     Printed in the United States of America
          1 3 5 7 9 10 8 6 4 2

I assure you I will be totally normal again as soon as the money gets here.

—Franziska zu Reventlow

A HISTORY OF MONEY

He hasn't yet turned fifteen when he sees his first dead person in the flesh. He's somewhat astonished that this man, a close family friend of his mother's husband, is as disagreeable to him now, shrunken by the too-narrow walls of his coffin, as when he was alive. He sees him in his suit, sees that face rejuvenated by the funeral preparations, made up, the skin yellowish and gleaming like wax, only flawless, and he feels the same rabid antipathy that comes over him every time their paths cross. But then it's always been like this, since the day he first met him, eight years earlier, one summer in Mar del Plata, a little before lunch.

There's no hint of a breeze, the cicadas are launching another deafening offensive. Fleeing the heat, the heat and the boredom, he wanders idly around the big, ramshackle house built at the beginning of the twentieth century where he never manages to find his place, despite the smiles the owners greet him with almost before he's set foot in it, the private room they assign to him on the first floor, and the insistence with which his mother assures him that, even though he's new there, he has just as much right to the house and to everything that's in it—including the garage full of bikes, surfboards, and polystyrene bodyboards, and also the garden with its linden trees, gazebo, swing seat, and flower beds full of hydrangeas that the sun scorches and discolors until the petals look as though they're made of paper—as everyone else, and by everyone else she means the still vague but inexplicably expanding legion that he, with a bewilderment that years of hearing the expression have not dissipated, hears called his stepfamily, a whole tribe of step-cousins, step-aunts, and step-grandmothers that have sprung up from one day to the next like warts, often without giving him time for the basics, like remembering their names, for example, and associating them with the corresponding faces. The agony he feels forced to suffer because he doesn't belong: every step he takes is wrong, every decision a mistake. To live is to regret.

At some point in his drifting he ends up on the ground floor and sees him, catches him, in fact—the dead man, of course, who else?—sneaking around in the dining room as though on tiptoe, acting suspiciously. He lacks the disturbing agility of a thief. If there's one thing he doesn't present, with his strawberry-blond hair, almost feminine air, and skin that's always flecked with red marks, it's a threat. He moves lightly, with the delicacy of a mime or a ballerina, taking a few silent leaps that are as inoffensive as the mission that's brought him to the dining room before the bell has officially announced lunchtime: to get an advantage on the rest of the family in plundering, one by one, with the tips of his manicured, methodical fingers, the little dishes on which the crostini that he decided to buy personally that morning, a brand with a vaguely foreign name whose goods, it seems, he has been praising for a week without anyone paying any attention, have just been served.

He trusted, as everybody does, that death would cleanse that old unease. That much at least, if it didn't manage to wipe it out entirely. And so he approaches the coffin, the only thing, apart from the dead man's wife—whom he also hasn't seen in a long while—that he's drawn to in this suffocating apartment his mother brought him to without saying a word as soon as he got home from school. He advances with his chin pressed against his chest, with the same grave, engrossed air that casts its shadow with rare unanimity over the adults' faces, which he's able to copy perfectly in less than ten minutes, just by glancing at it, further emboldened by the formality of the school uniform his mother forced him to keep on, the only thing his wardrobe offered to match the solemnity of the occasion. But when he arrives at the casket, hoping that seeing the dead man live and in person—as he's sometimes joked about with those schoolmates who share his inexperience in the matter of wakes—will banish his former hostility to the cellar where his childhood intolerances are withering away, the voices around him merge into a confused murmur, the ambient sound disappears, and he discovers, to his incredulity, that the only thing he can hear, and once again he hears the whole thing, preserved in a state of total purity, is the intolerable crackling of crostini in the dead man's mouth. In fact, it's two alternating sounds: the clear but flat crunch of the crostini as they're ground up by the teeth, muffled by the propriety of an educated mouth that opens itself as little as possible while it chews, and a sharp, regular smacking, like tiny lashes from a whip that resound at the moment of pulverization, when the lips delight in prolonging the pleasure of tasting for a few seconds more. But no: they're not in the air or in his head. They're not a hallucination or a memory. They're there, ringing right inside the dead man's mouth.

How many more times does he meet him over the course of the following years? Ten? Thirty times? And still nothing stays with him as much as that repulsive crackling. He sees the dead man almost every summer in Mar del Plata, and in a great variety of situations: in his swimsuit, for example, with his very white, mole-speckled skin scorched by the sun, walking toward the sea with his feet spread out in a V like a duck, or showing off his salmon-colored shirts in an Italian convertible in which he's said to have tried his luck once or twice at the racetrack, or taking a beating at golf and getting distracted—his little pencil barely acknowledging the seven ridiculous swings he just had to use on a par-four—by the way he says a seam on the glove he ends up relinquishing tickles his wrist, by the slightly blunt point of the tee he puts between his teeth or the hunger he began to feel just after ten o'clock in the morning, trivial matters that he discusses loudly as if they were episodes in an ominous drama, sometimes over the course of entire holes, with the sole aim of putting his opponents off their game and so perhaps making up for the unfortunate numbers on his card. He sees him in Buenos Aires, too, in his own house, as a guest at some family birthday wandering around with the slightly insolent superiority of those family friends who claim a deeper intimacy than relatives themselves, and signing checks in a café on Calle Florida, one of the huge, old-fashioned salons with lavishly upholstered seats and dourly professional waiters where, under the pretext of familiarizing him with a type of adult life that will always be strange to him, his mother's husband often has lunch and closes deals with his colleagues. He sees him one sunny day on a farm outside the city, wearing white pants and riding boots, holding a long glass containing a liquid the color of cherries that he drinks in short sips, almost sniffing it, as if it were very hot, while a very thin servant in a cap stands to one side, waiting uncomfortably for something that never happens.

But what has remained with him ever since is not the high-pitched tone of his voice, nor his fragile, constantly raw temper, nor the air of self-importance with which he takes a glass of wine by the stem and swirls it on the armrest of his chair. It's not his sunglasses, not the pale cotton sweaters he ties around his neck, not his loafers with buckles or the variety of tense impatience that characterizes his relationships with other people and with the world, two things or categories of things whose existence he accepts only through clenched teeth, as though they existed solely to waste his time, especially any social inferiors who happen to get in his way, farmhands, caddies, chauffeurs, waiters, and above all the select army of maids who patrol the house in Mar del Plata at all hours, and who every day, during lunch and dinner, serve up on gleaming little stainless-steel plates the crostini that he ends up instituting after lauding them for a whole summer, which will accompany every meal in the house from then on, having dethroned the water biscuits. Ever since that summer lunchtime in Mar del Plata, the thing that has immediately identified the dead man, at least for him, as surely as a scar and so magically that he doesn't even need to be making it any longer for him to feel it filling his ears like a poison, is the sound his mouth makes when he chews those fucking crostini.

He doesn't want to lean over the coffin for fear that he'll find a crumb stuck in the corner of his lips. That would be too much. He's right there, three paces away, now entering the orbit of the crackling but thinking what he wouldn't give to be somewhere else—ensconced in a cinema, for example, watching one of the Czech or Hungarian films nobody will go see with him at the Communist Party theater, or even just in the room next door, watching like a stowaway from some ignominious hiding place as the dead man's widow succumbs to the influence of the sedatives, lies down on a bed that's overflowing with jackets, stretches out those long, bony legs he knows so well, and takes off her high heels with the tips of her toes—and stirring inside him he can feel the same unease he always felt during those lunches in Mar del Plata, when the dead man, talking continuously as ever, as though delivering a monologue, apparently the only style of dialogue he knows, shoved one crostini after another into his mouth.

If he'd even restricted himself to that, to chewing them with the patience of an epicurean rodent who uses the crackling as the sound track to its harangues. But no: he also has to relish the feast to which he's just treated himself, opening and closing his lips as delightedly as a newborn. This unease is as intense as that one; it erases, empties the scene of everything else, everything that distinguishes this moment from those earlier ones and underpins this muffled, slightly underwater world of the fellowship of mourning: the creak of the parquet beneath his trespassing feet, the sweet scent coming from the wreaths of flowers, the shadows filled with sobbing, and even the question that has been circulating constantly, like an open secret, since the early morning when the team of police divers found the dead man at the bottom of the San Antonio River: *Where is the money?* Beyond any of that, though, what this old unease obscures for him is the terrible evidence that the crostini lover is dead, as mute and rigid as any other dead person, and the flavor of those tiny pieces of toast that drove him crazy with pleasure while he was alive is now as far from his reach as everything else that is of this world, most obviously his two children—the elder of whom is being kept in the kitchen, bribed with a glass of chocolate milk that he refuses to try, while the younger, who's months old, sleeps in a bedroom under the watch of a maid—and his widow, with her black eyes, her always slightly chapped lips, her milky skin, and her constellations of freckles.

In fact, what this feeling of unease brings back to him is a whole class ritual. Lunchtime is the platform that the dead man uses to play at politics, which in his case, obsessed as he is with the only tragic injustice to which he appears to have any sensitivity—the unequal struggle between vulgarity and good taste—means denouncing the garish orange they've decided to paint the traditionally white wicker seats at the beach club, or the streets flooded with music for servants, or the plebeian indecency that has infected the titles of the plays showing over the summer. Less out of politeness than a determination to convince, the dead man looks his interlocutors in the eye while he rants. He passes gracefully from one to the next, committed to winning them over to a cause they have little interest in, and which sooner or later they'll renounce, having been overwhelmed by a vehemence they have difficulty sharing. And while he speaks, his fingers begin to move, blindly but surely tracing lines of latitude on the tablecloth until they stop next to the little stainless-steel plate, where they catch the edge of the crostini on top of the pile and carry it to his mouth. The operation has a light, almost calligraphic elegance, though the dead man has achieved this only recently, after days of practice. As well as being crispy, the crostini are made of an exceptionally fine substance, and the pores it breathes through give them a vertiginous fragility. They disintegrate on the slightest contact, and once broken they're worthless. How many times, early on, does he misjudge their consistency—the dead man himself, who declares them a miracle of delicacy while reviling the boorish rusticity of water biscuits—and smash them to pieces no sooner than he's ripped off their cellophane wrapping, or shatter them while lifting them to his mouth, or make them explode the moment he bites into them, so that an hour and a half later, when lunch is finished and he finally stands up, the proportion he's managed to get into his stomach is ridiculous compared with the detritus that covers his section of the tablecloth.

Sometimes, seeing him like this, talking and chewing constantly, he doesn't know what holds him back, what formidable force stops him from reacting, from standing on his seat, getting the red corduroy of the upholstery dirty with his muddy shoes, jumping on the table, trampling dishes, steaming plates, and the white-linen tablecloth fresh from the dry cleaner's, and launching himself in a suicidal attack on the dead man, shutting him up by taking a knife to his throat, smashing his teeth in, or cutting out his tongue. But time and again, he sits quietly on his chair, his arms falling to his sides, his eyes fixed on a meal he'll barely touch, while the voice of the dead man and the crunching of the crostini keep weaving their hateful wilderness around him. What else can he do, at his age, and in this enemy territory where not even his mother manages to find her footing—his mother, the one who takes him and leaves him there, swearing and perjuring herself that he has nothing to fear. Fasting: that is his only form of protest. Fasting and, two hours later, in the middle of the siesta, going down to the kitchen, famished, and stealing a stock of water biscuits in a commando raid to gorge himself on with slices of *queso fresco* alone in his room, with the blinds pulled low and the bedside lamp spitting its solitary cone of light onto a comic book. Fasting and waiting in silence, with his suitcase mentally packed and his heart pounding, for the first of February to come once and for all, so that his father will take him on holiday far, very far away from there, it doesn't matter where.

As if that were possible. Because there is no escape, not in space or in time. The proof is that eight years later, when the crostini lover is lying faceup with his hands crossed on his chest, and he is fourteen years old, all of his hormones at war and no obligation, now, to sit down at any table in any enemy territory, the music that fills his ears is not the grandiose trumpets of "Jerusalem," the song that opens *Brain Salad Surgery*, the Emerson, Lake & Palmer CD that he spends hours listening to, locked in his bedroom, but the crunching of the dead man's jaws showing no mercy to those fucking crostini. In fact, it's around this magnetic sound, which he could single out and recognize anywhere, like an epileptic detecting the peculiar atmospheric conditions that foreshadow a fit, that he has, over the years, absorbed and organized everything he's learned about the man from others or through firsthand observation, things he probably notices and remembers only because they come to him associated with, forever fused with that crackling sound, and the crackling, in turn, with the gust of unease that unfailingly assails him, and then with the urge to get up from his seat, jump on the table, put a knife to the dead man's throat, et cetera. It's this sound that comes to him when anyone mentions the dead man's name in conversation, this sound that eclipses all others, including the din of the cicadas, when he leans out the window of his room in the mansion in Mar del Plata and sees the notorious Italian convertible coming to a halt in front of the closed door; that forces itself upon him every time he arrives home from school to find, scattered all over the house, the signs that betray his presence, convincing him to go to his room by the route on which he's sure to avoid meeting him: the blue blazer with its gold badge hanging from the back of a chair, the packet of cigarettes with the solid-silver Dupont lighter on top, and the reddish-brown leather attaché case with his initials burned into the skin, branding-style, which he always carries with him, which they say he was also carrying with him the morning he boarded the helicopter heading to Villa Constitución, and of which there is no trace whatsoever when, after combing half the delta, the four police divers finally find the helicopter and bodies at the bottom of the San Antonio River. Vaporized, disappeared in a puff of smoke, along with everything that is believed to have been inside it, papers, documentation, pay stubs, checks, and, most important, the bundle of money entrusted to him that morning to be taken to the plant in Zárate, undeclared money, obviously, given the rather underhand ends for which it's destined, though its presence in the attaché case is confirmed in low voices by a couple of employees of the powerful iron-and-steel company he works for, which has been hit for more than three weeks by a union conflict and is now disrupted by sudden stoppages in production, by the election by absolute majority of an internal committee that's redder than the blood that will soon flow, by threats to seize the plant for an indeterminate period, and by the death in rather mysterious circumstances of one of the conflict's key figures, the only person capable of either resolving or detonating it.

How those last few days of January drag. At times, as a very young boy, intrigued by the way in which fifteen minutes on the clock can pass in slow motion or in the blink of an eye according to the time of day, the situation, the people he happens to be with, the weather, the light, his mood, the activities to come or just past, it occurs to him that maybe time isn't universal at all but rather supremely subjective, a sort of local good that each family and each house and even each person produces in their own way, with their own methods and instruments, and in the most literal sense of producing, investing physical strength, labor, raw materials, everything that the evanescent consistency of time would seem to make irrelevant, as if it were more a domestic craft than the elusive passage that everyone insists it is.

As soon as the last week of January begins, the world gets heavier, and the hours begin to crawl along, gasping, as though climbing an endless hill. Rather than bringing the next one along, each day is an obstacle that delays and conceals it. Eventually time stops altogether—real time, whose passage he notices only for the way it draws in the only thing he wants in the world, to leave Mar del Plata once and for all, and with it the crackling of the crostini in the dead man's mouth, the mansion, the requirement to be silent during siestas, the boredom of those lunches and dinners at which he invariably stays mute and almost stationary, intimidated by the rules of an etiquette he doesn't understand and by the extravagant variety of cutlery laid out beside his plate, which he has no idea how or when to use, even though more than once, at the height of his torpor, shaken by the impulse to do something, anything, to dispel the clouds of drowsiness, he suddenly begins to classify them, reordering them by size, color, and shine, or uses them to draw lines in the white-linen tablecloth, until someone—never his mother, who took the decision from the word go to turn a blind eye when it comes to family-law disputes, but rather some member of his so-called stepfamily, a step-grandmother, step-uncle, or even the step-cousin who, though hardly a year or two older than him, speaks to him with incontestable authority, like a lieutenant to a private—scolds him from the other end of the table. Because the other time, the one that's marked by the clock, the succession of meals and outfits, the sun's work on skin, the bodies bathed, or the tiredness on people's faces, the time that seems to advance, dragged along by the more or less regular meter of the days, has been reduced to a mere formality, a fiction intended to hide the paralysis of things.

The only relief comes from the safe-conduct that will get him out of there. The two bus tickets, his and his father's, which he keeps himself, in his own hands. He can't wait. He won't even allow his father to buy them and bring them when he comes to fetch him at the gate of the mansion in Mar del Plata every February 1, as dictated by the equitable summer schedule—January for her, February for him—his parents draw up a few months after they separate, by common agreement, as they say, if it's fair to call common an agreement orchestrated by the lawyer of just one of the parties, hers, under which his mother, making a show of a fortitude and conviction that she doesn't possess, sets the agenda, and his father complies without objection, cowed by the same mixture of weariness, incompetence, and guilt with which he left the family home, renouncing his right to a lawyer, to his share of the blue 1957 Auto Unión, and to his percentage of the second-floor walk-up where they have lived together for a little more than two nightmarish years—both wedding gifts from his father-in-law—but not to the money with which his father-in-law entices him to leave the family home, which it would seem he needs to pay a backlog of debts.

He's overcome by impatience. As the day of the journey draws near—it's the middle of the month, and a new set of holidaymakers is arriving—he worries that they'll run out of tickets and the trip will have to be postponed. And so he goes to buy them himself, in person, much too far in advance, from the bus station in Mar del Plata. The first few times, his mother goes with him. He's old enough to understand the whole process perfectly, and the order it comes in—father, leave, travel, bus, ticket, buy—but he's still so small that even on tiptoe he can't maneuver his head into the ticket vendor's line of vision. Later he goes by himself, on his bicycle, happy because this way—without witnesses—the idea of escaping Mar del Plata gains an invigorating dose of illegitimacy, even though it's his mother who pays for the tickets and chooses which bus they'll take; but also with his heart in his mouth, steering the bicycle with one hand and using the other, shoved as deep as it'll go into his pocket, to count the bills two or three times per block to reassure himself that he hasn't lost one.

Those newly bought tickets are guarded, kept like a secret. He takes them everywhere with him, into town, to the cinema, on bike rides and expeditions to abandoned lots, even to the restaurants by the port that he sometimes goes to with his stepfamily, proto–theme parks in which a couple of anchors, a few miserable buoys, some fishing rods hanging from the ceiling, and two or three drunk-looking papier-mâché sailors watching over the dining rooms are intended to capture the maritime world to which their menus—always limited to the same handful of options: mussels Provençal, sole meunière, langoustine—are also an insult, and where the

dead man gets up to his old tricks, rebuking the waiters before he's even sat down for the scandal of a breadbasket that's
overflowing with buns, kaiser rolls, bread sticks, and water
biscuits, but that still lacks his favorite crostini, an oversight
he takes personally, like a direct provocation, and which is
sufficient cause for him to add the establishment to his ever-
longer blacklist of restaurants. He disregards his mother, who
tells him there's no better place to lose them, and takes them
to the beach, even though they force him to forgo his bathing
suit—in whose pockets he might put them and then, at any
moment, succumb to distraction, forget that he has them, and
take them into the sea with him, with predictably horren-
dous consequences—and to roast in his pants at ninety-five
degrees in the shade, condemned to contemplate the water
from afar. He even keeps them with him while he sleeps, but
not in his pajama pockets, where they'd be liable to fall out or
be stolen by some stealthy person during the night. He keeps
them clutched in his fist like a lucky charm, so that when the
day finally comes, they've been folded and unfolded so many
times, stuffed so deeply in his pockets, subjected to so much
grazing and fondling, hidden in so many impregnable ref-
uges, that the departure date and time and the seat numbers
and even the name of the bus company are barely legible.
This is the sorry state they're in the afternoon he finally walks
out the door of the mansion in Mar del Plata carrying his little
navy-blue suitcase—alone, as he always insists to his mother,
less out of a desire to be independent than to deny her those
last twenty meters, which he's convinced she would use to try
to dissuade him from going, something she is very far from
wanting to do, so thrilled is she by the prospect of a whole
month off the job of being a mother—and then walks the long
gravel path that leads to the street, clambers up onto the stone
wall that extends from the front gate, and, still holding his
suitcase, settles down to wait for his father to arrive.

It's one of those radiant, perfectly idyllic days with no clouds or wind that are the reason summer exists, and nobody wants to waste it. Apart from him, and he's not sorry. A blind joy swells his chest, leaving him breathless. He watches the procession of families passing by on their way to the beach, umbrellas, deck chairs, and polystyrene coolers in tow, delighted at the prospect of hours of sun, and notes the sorrowful look they all give him when they see him waiting by the gate, dressed from head to toe in street clothes and carrying a suitcase, like an orphan or some kind of invalid who's forbidden to go to the beach. He scorns them silently. He compares his happiness at the thought that in just half an hour he will be with his father, on board the bus to Villa Gesell, with the banal enthusiasm on those faces that will return in two or three hours charred by the sun, and he feels like the luckiest person on earth. But fifteen minutes go by, and then twenty, and then another twenty-five, and he realizes with a faint shudder that he has exhausted the games he'd been using to distract himself from his impatience. He's already massacred the trail of ants that had managed to scale his bare thigh and carry their cargo of leaves to the other side. He's messed with the leaves of the privet that crowns the stone wall so much he's practically pruned it. He's sung, he's counted—cars with even and odd license plates, bicycles, stray dogs, seconds— and he's been wiping the snot from his nose and expertly, without even looking, sticking it all on the wall, sealing the slight indent that separates the blocks of stone. Half an hour passes: no sign of his father.

At one point he turns and looks behind him, toward the house, and, after making sure that his mother isn't stationed at a window, watching him, he gets down from the wall, still clutching his suitcase, and approaches the edge of the sidewalk, then looks as far as he can down the sloping street his father appears on every summer, always little by little, like a survivor emerging disheveled but proud from some abyss, head first, bald, roasted, gleaming, with its two strips of curly hair growing carelessly at the sides, then shoulders, then his torso in a freshly laundered shirt. But he peers down a whole scorched block of heat haze, and all he can make out is an intimate congress of two ice cream vendors who have crossed the trunks of their tricycles in the afternoon sun and are counting the money they've made over the course of this magnificent day, and perhaps lamenting the fact that they've already run out of merchandise, at barely five past four, with at least two or three good hours of selling left.

With a pang of desperation, never taking his eyes from the deserted street, because there's nothing he fears more than what he might find if he turned back toward the house now (his mother's sympathy, the merciful, nunnish solidarity with which she opens her arms to offer him asylum, and the sequence of hurdles awaiting him a little later on: the gate, and the gravel path, and the house, and his private room on the first floor, whose papered walls covered with life preservers and anchors, nautical knots, an ape dressed as a sailor—childish, pastel versions of the motifs that decorate the restaurants by the port—he knows and hates from memory), he searches for the tickets, unfolds them on his thigh, and tries to find the departure time in the puzzle of dates and numbers that the tickets have always been, but which he's only noticing now, precisely when he most needs them to be clean and legible, and for a moment he only has eyes for the one thing that would relieve him, any number higher than four, whether it's the date or the bus number or the company's phone number or the arrival time. But eventually he finds the departure time, he finds the words *departure time* and reads *four* and he feels as though he's dying.

He feels as though he's dying. Everything stops moving around him, like a liquid losing its fizz and falling into a solid, permanent repose. He's still facing the sloping road, down which a ball spat out of a neighboring garden starts to bounce, so he can't see the house, but he can feel it, he can sense the shape of the porch, the slightly jagged outline of the façade. He considers running away. Anything, he thinks, but go back. Then he hears his mother's voice calling to him from the other side of the gate: "There must have been some problem," she says dismissively, as though trying to play it down: "He'll be here soon. Come here, let's wait for him inside." He turns around and starts to go back. His mother opens the gate for him, and to his ears the creaking of the rusty hinges sounds like the steps that lead to the gallows. When he reaches the familiar, shifting surface of the gravel, he can't take any more, and he bursts into tears. His mother puts a hand on his shoulder, a light hand that's intended to go unnoticed. She's tactful enough not to hug him. She knows he couldn't bear it. But even so, he shakes off her arm and walks on, crying. And when he sees the huge bulk of the mansion in front of him, almost falling on top of him, he hears an unmistakable voice behind him, shouting his name.

He turns around and looks at his father, stunned. He doesn't recognize him. He doesn't know who he is, why he's smiling at him like that, what could compel him to put that leather bag on the ground and open his arms and stretch them out toward him, inviting him to run up and hug him. It's past four in the afternoon, and there's no reason for his father to exist anymore. They've missed the bus, the trip's a lost cause, and his father—along with everything associated with him in the possible world that's just been obliterated by his lateness: the sand dunes on the north beach; the Croatian guesthouse; pancakes after the beach; mighty defecations in the pine forests; nocturnal pinball, table football, and go-karting marathons in the Combo Park on Avenida Tres—must have vanished too, irretrievably. The idea that once one possibility has been lost and another might spring up and replace it is a late conquest of the imagination. He hasn't crossed that threshold yet. For him, a possibility is always just one possibility: if it ceases to exist as a possibility, the world that accompanied it must also cease to exist, entirely and forever.

So he no longer has a father. He won't have one until thirty seconds later, an interval he spends imagining and getting used to the idea of his life from that moment on; not only his immediate life, in which he'll no doubt be condemned once more to the four walls of the mansion in Mar del Plata, but also everything that will follow, going back to school and seeing his classmates again, all exactly the same while he's a hundred percent different, and the moment during one recess, which he's already glimpsing with an almost painful excitement, when he allows himself the pleasure of delivering the bombshell: I don't have a father anymore. But in spite of all this, thirty seconds later that man is still there, standing with his arms open and smiling for some invisible photographer, still claiming the rights he's just lost, above all the right to look at him and make direct contact with him, as if there were nothing separating them, not air, nor the shadows of trees, nor the blinding reflections of the sun, nor the dust that's sometimes raised by the wind when it swirls around the entrance to the house, and of course not his mother, with whom he hasn't exchanged a look or even a word since he arrived, not even to agree to the essential technical details—the date of their return, sun protection, food, his toothbrush, the benefits of bathing with some degree of regularity—which his father can usually only bring himself to consider at the last minute, with one foot on the bus, and always reluctantly, as though by considering them he were ceding to the will of a woman who, even though she can't bear him, even though she refuses to say his name and forbids him to come upstairs when he comes to fetch him from the apartment on

Ortega y Gasset, insists on keeping him and delaying his departure every February 1. And not only is he still there, he's also smiling and telling him in his most peremptory tone not to be like that, that there's no need to "get worked up." That yes, they have indeed missed the four o'clock bus, but that they can miss the next one, at four thirty, too, and the next, and five, twenty, a hundred more buses, they can miss every bus in the terminal at Mar del Plata and in every bus terminal in the world. Because they, he—he points to him with his index finger, the same finger that one Saturday morning a few years earlier took a line of foam from his own face and put it on the end of his nose while he stood beside him, looking up at him shaving—and he—and he points to his own chest with the same finger, to the very center of the V formed by the two panels of his unbuttoned shirt—*they* can go to Villa Gesell when they like, whenever they feel like it, whenever it suits them. Right now, if they want to: all they have to do is put one foot on the street and that's it, they're already on their way. Because they, he says, aren't taking the bus to Villa Gesell. They're taking a taxi.

It's 103 kilometers away. He doesn't know that, of course. Not in those terms, anyway. But whatever he lacks in the way of conventional measurements he makes up for with a certain awareness of proportion, and he knows that any journey that's usually taken by long-distance bus, no matter how decrepit and slow the bus is, or how many times it stops en route, cannot be translated to any other form of wheeled transport—apart from your own car, and, as far as he knows, his father doesn't have his own car, he hasn't had one since he relinquished the blue Auto Unión, whose congested motor he still seems to hear sometimes in his dreams, and he isn't considering getting another, as he frequently promises, always in a loud voice and with the emphatic conviction of a militant, confident that this snub will be enough to bring down the entire automotive industry; and in fact he doesn't have another until two or three years later, when the need to please a girlfriend who can't stand going on vacation on public transport compels him to buy a cream-colored secondhand Fiat 600. A bus's relation to a taxi, or more to the point its lack of relation, its striking incommensurability, seems to him the same as that of a plane to a bicycle, for example, or an ocean liner to one of the inflatable mattresses on which he likes to travel very slowly from one end of swimming pools to the other with his eyes half closed.

In a fraction of a second, everything shifts backward and speeds up. He goes to his mother, takes back his case with a yank while giving her a quick kiss, runs to his father and takes his hand (the hug is saved for later, for when his father is really his father again), and they step down into the street together. Walking backward, in the same direction as the advancing cars but facing them, as though he's not prepared to lose a second more, his father stretches out an arm, stops the first taxi (which brakes with customary precision, delivering the back door's handle directly to him), pushes his son into the backseat, and, after piling up their luggage on the front seat, sits beside him. Then, agitated and rapidly rolling down his window, he gives the order, "To Villa Gesell."

In 1966, in Argentina, the only people who would take a taxi on a 103-kilometer journey between resorts on a potholed road with no shoulder and no service stations, which is fed by tributary streams of bicycles, cars without lights, trucks with ravaged steering columns, and other mortal threats, are taxi drivers on vacation, people running away from the police, and compulsive gamblers drunk on the euphoria of an unexpectedly prosperous night at the casino. His father, who as far as he knows is none of these things, for the moment at least, though that might change, dives headfirst into that Rambler while it stands boiling in the sun of the most perfect day of the summer; he doesn't ask any questions, not even whether the journey he's just requested is actually possible, whether the taxi driver will accept it or not, or, most important, whether he has enough money to cover it. He takes all that as given, as though it had already happened. In fact, nobody devotes a single word to the matter during the entire journey. Certainly not his father, who now, after a whole month away from his son, wants to make up for lost time and find out about everything he's done in his absence. Nor him, not a word. The prodigious recklessness that had captivated him a moment earlier now frightens him. He thinks that if he says anything, if he mentions what has just happened, even if only to confirm that it really happened and relive the elation he felt while it was happening, what happened might stop happening, history might retreat and everything disappear and return to nothing. And while all this goes on and he hears himself recounting the minutiae of his summer, pausing on the dead man, on his boundless passion for those crostini and above all on the repulsive noise he makes while he chews them—a detail that his father celebrates with a loud burst of laughter that's inspired by vanity more than real appreciation or entertainment, so proud is he that his son, at six years old and in the heart of his stepfamily, has used the gift for microscopic observation he says has always characterized the men of the family, even though an important part of that lineage, his own father, used that gift, in which he seems to have excelled, to make his son's life a true nightmare—his attention keeps wandering off entirely, attracted by the ticking of the taxi's meter, on which the slides have started to fall, they're falling, they will continue to fall, he thinks, for a long time, for the whole unheard-of eternity known as 103 kilometers, and they won't stop until they've reached who knows what number.

He doesn't have the faintest idea. Now, with the dead man's face so near and another expansive wave of crostini-crackling assailing him, he can't help but ask himself how much money there was in the attaché case of which there's no news even when the police divers find the helicopter and the bodies at the bottom of the river, how much and, crucially, why the dead man was asked to take that money to the plant at Zárate in person, whether it's to pay the supplementary under-the-table fee the police want to charge for carrying out the suppression agreed on by the management and the local heads of the force, or to placate the workers with a pay raise that will distract them from the radical demands they're being pushed toward by the red faction of the union leadership, which plays an all-or-nothing game, or even to bribe the red faction of the leadership directly and resolve the whole matter without a bloodbath. But what he'd really like right now is to be able to remember how much the taxi ride to Villa Gesell cost. No hope: it's a total blank. What he does know is that it's the first large sum of money he's aware of, or the first time he's aware that money can be a large sum. Until then it was always small, portable, just another thing among many, only touched by a sort of ancient magic wand—so ancient that the few people who have seen it in action are dead—that gives it its ability to overpower everything else, to *eat it up*; the exact power he discovers his pieces wield over enemy pieces and vice versa a little later in front of a chessboard in the dining room of the Croatian hotel he dreams of while traveling by taxi to Villa Gesell. By taxi, to Villa Gesell, while outside the world keeps stupidly turning, indifferent to this feat.

But what relation can there be between the kind of money capable of eating up a bar of milk chocolate, a packet of baseball cards, an eraser, or the bus ticket to Villa Gesell that's now going through its death throes at the bottom of his pants' pocket, and the money you'd need to get together in order to eat up something invisible, something as out of scale as those 103 kilometers to Villa Gesell? He's seen money, of course. At the age of six he has even lent it. He has what he calls *my safe*, an old first-aid box with a cracked red cross and a loose lid, in which he keeps his capital, coins, small or torn notes, change that his mother and his mother's husband and even his father sometimes let him keep. It's to him and his safe—which infuses his money with the smell of bandages, adhesive tape, and Merthiolate while it sleeps—that his mother turns when she needs change for a tip or some small expense, which happens more often than she would like but still always takes her by surprise and fills her with a dramatic sense of adversity, setting her hurriedly rummaging in her purse while the doorman, the newsstand guy, or the grocery store's delivery boy stand waiting, until she comes up with nothing, not a single coin. His safe: how he treasures those casual donations when he gets them, and how little he seems to remember receiving them later on, when, the fourth or fifth time his mother asks him for a loan—she's always short of change, though it's impossible not to be in a city and a country where small sums of money are and always will be precious commodities—he delights in reminding her of all those she has yet to repay— every single one to date—and warns her to settle her account.

How much. He starts wondering even while he sits in the backseat of the taxi, curled up against his father, who has rolled his window all the way down and is sticking out a defiant arm that's perfectly browned before his vacation has even begun. He looks at the meter hanging on the taxi's console and allows himself to be entranced by the mechanical regularity with which those ancient numbers, already ancient even then, replace one another in the machine's two little windows, like candidates voluntarily renouncing a starring role—that of the definitive figure for the journey—even though nobody has taken the trouble to judge or reject them. If only he knew, he could lose himself in what will later be one of his favorite pastimes (which he puts to use every time he has to pay for any countable goods): prorating. He could prorate the total cost of the journey according to the minutes taken, and know the price of not only the 103 kilometers to Villa Gesell, but also each kilometer, or the time the Rambler takes to cover each kilometer. But he doesn't know. He won't know until an hour and forty-five minutes later, when they arrive in Villa Gesell and the taxi parks outside the hotel run by Croatians, and his father, with the remarkable dexterity picked up who knows where that gives his gestures a prodigious insouciance, as if he were performing them in a medium with no possible obstacles—air or water—puts a hand in his pocket and pulls out the wad of notes to pay.

He's awed by the wad: just the naked wad, no wallet nor one of the elegant clasps that he sees many years later in a TV series that reconstructs with insane attention to detail the period when he and his father traveled by taxi to Villa Gesell—the same period, if you can call it that, only in the middle of New York, in the ghetto inhabited by a few pioneers of depredation who, meager as they are, and even conscious of their own irredeemable mediocrity, can already see how far the world will pass into their possession in the years to come. The characters using the clasp are successful forty-somethings dressed exactly like his father, in tweed checked jackets, white shirts always fresh from the laundromat, and ankle boots with buckles on the side, and all of them have his father's unfailing complicity with their pants' pockets, which makes it seem less like the pockets were designed for their hands and more the other way around, their hands for these pockets. How many notes must there be? Forty? Fifty? Folded in two, with the largest on the outside and the smallest on the inside, always in strictly decreasing order (and one last slot on the inside, after the smallest notes, reserved for his true monetary weakness: foreign currency, predominantly dollars, Swiss francs, pounds sterling, lire, whichever he's handled most lately at the travel agency where he works), the wad is so bulky that when he's holding it his father can't close his hand, he can't even put the tips of his fingers together. And it's heavy, as heavy as a thing, a solid, not just the pile of printed papers it actually is.

So they've arrived, and it's time to pay. Overcome by a rush of fear, he starts to shrink into his corner of the backseat, a paradise of fragrant pleather where he's just spent almost two happy hours enjoying the pioneer's brazen sense of superiority (other people swim the English Channel, he unites Mar del Plata and Villa Gesell in a taxi!), but which his terror now transforms into a suffocating hell, a stew of heat and the purring of the motor and the smell of burnt gasoline. He thinks: What if there isn't enough money? Because his father might have miscalculated. He might simply not have calculated, eager to make up for the disappointment caused by his late arrival and the missed bus. But he soon sees him lean forward, put a forearm on the back of the seat, and take a closer look at the meter, where the now still numbers are offering their final verdict, and his father's direct approach to the situation calms him somewhat. Everything happens very quickly. The taxi driver leans over, notes the figure on the meter, and starts to look for its monetary equivalent on a plastic tariff sheet. There's an identical sheet hanging from the back of the seat on their side, but once again his father decides to ignore it: when it comes to reckoning accounts, he trusts his brain's skill and speed more than the verdict of a printed form, especially one jointly produced by the taxi drivers' union and the Ministry of Transport, both nerve centers of swindling. And in this particular instance, he also knows full well that there is no tariff to cover something as unscripted as a Mar del Plata–Villa Gesell. It's a silent, pathetic duel. The taxi driver's rheumatic finger is still quivering in a wilderness of red and black numbers, hunting a figure it'll never find, when his father announces the definitive price in a low voice, as though to himself, or for an invisible but very close witness, then selects five or six notes, separates them from the wad, and pays.

Nobody counts money like his father. Counts in the sense of accounting, which when it comes to his father—a man who went to a technical school and graduated with just one skill, a rare talent for what he himself calls *numbers*, which he flaunts rather immodestly in public, the only thing he permits himself to boast about (being enemy number one of all vainglory)—means purely mental calculations, in which the use of any supplementary instrument is forbidden, including taxi tariff sheets, naturally, but, moreover, machines, calculators, abacuses, manual counters, to say nothing of the electronic bill-counters the size of espresso machines or water dispensers that, years later, are made so trendy by inflation and the foreign-currency black market, machines produced by Galantz and Elwic, MF Pluses by Cirilo Ayling, pride of Argentina—prosthetics that represent the worst, the lowest rank of human spinelessness and dependency—and also pencil and paper and even so-called natural mechanisms like fingers. But also *counts* in the sense of physical action, as in counting notes. He's struck by this at a very early age, one day when he spends an afternoon off school accompanying his father on his rounds through the city's business district, where he works, and sees him cashing checks at banks, buying tickets at airline offices, and trading foreign currency at currency exchanges, and he will never cease to be struck by it, even in the last days at the hospital forty-two years later, just before the lung failure that condemns him to an oxygen mask and tubes, when his father selects two fifty-peso notes from an already significantly depleted wad, having decided to give them as a tip, "before it's too late," in his words, to the morning nurse, who surprises him by speaking German to him while changing his IV, giving him an injection, or taking his temperature. Nobody else has his aplomb, his proud, elegant efficiency, which transform the act of paying into one of sovereignty and are enough to make you forget that in truth it's always a secondary, reactive act. When he counts money, it's as if he were counting it simply to count it, for love of the art, as they say: because of the beauty of it, never because the logic of the transaction requires it of him. He never slips up, never lets one note stick to another or get stuck or folded, not to mention tear. His fingers are always dry—if he occasionally wets the tips with his tongue, which he says is a habit of bad bank cashiers, dishonest shopkeepers, and misers, it's always in mockery, just as he mocks the tricks people use to make up for abilities they naturally lack, and he always caricatures the ritual, giving it a bad actor's pompous gestures—and they move nimbly, without hesitating or pausing; on the very rare occasions on which they stop and start again, either because something else has distracted them or because they've been dizzied by their own speed and got lost, they resume the operation just as coolly as before, as though nothing had ever happened, like a musician taking up a score again at the phrase that tripped him up and playing on.

Unlike his rivals in the art of counting—cashiers, people who work at currency exchanges or in the money market, even his own colleagues at the travel agency—whose fingertips are black by the end of the day, tanned like leather by the layer of grime left by the money they've been handling all day, his father can count notes for hours without getting his fingers dirty. Even the rubber bands that fasten folded wads of notes—which his father always maneuvers with the fingers of one hand, like a one-armed juggler—lose their propensity for stickiness and dirt in his hands. It's as though money leaves no mark on him whatsoever. As soon as he thinks that phrase, he feels as though it's not the first time he's heard it, and he realizes that if it sounds familiar, that's because it isn't his.

He has heard it often from his mother's mouth, though she doesn't necessarily mean the same thing by it as he does. In fact, it's this very phrase that she uses a month later, when he returns from his February in Villa Gesell to the apartment on Ortega y Gasset—so tan that when he stands barefoot against the wall for her to measure how many centimeters he's grown while he was away from her, as she always does and always will, his feet would be lost against the dark wood floor if it weren't for his toenails, which shine like ten little luminous blots—and, showing off a capacity for memory that's as merciless as that of an abused woman, which his mother likes to do whenever she recalls the last time she saw him before his father took him away, she abruptly takes up the story of the missed bus and the taxi ride and says how nice, that if they went around spending it like that—paying three hundred for something any father with any sense of responsibility would have gotten for twenty by arriving on time for a meeting arranged months in advance—*anyone* would be immune to the marks of money. But isn't that what she herself does years later, when, in one brief, sparkling decade of celebration, ambition, and bad business, she squanders the small fortune that she inherits from her own father?

Meanwhile, he has to wash his hands every time he handles money. When he's at the zoo, for example, on one of the sessions of animal observation and sketching that often fill his Saturday mornings. He decides to buy a packet of the little cookies for animals, in the shape of animals, that are his downfall, and which he usually finishes in the blink of an eye, first the bears, his favorites, then the monkeys, the tapirs, the crocodiles, and so on, until the bottom of the packet is a morgue full of horrifying stumps: an elephant's trunk, a *pecarí*'s hoof, the spiral tail of a pig. For a moment he feels like he's taken a terrifyingly bold step, like crossing a frontier from which nobody ever returns, or at least not in the same form they left in. He asks himself what will become of a boy fed on cookies for animals in the shape of animals. And while he's thinking about it, he puts the change from the cookies in a pocket—the route varies, as do the animals he sketches, but the one rule on every visit to the zoo is the agreement he has with his father, who goes with him, that he pays for everything he eats there himself, with his own money—and returns to the enormous, exhausting white page he's just spread out on top of his drawing case. He's only just begun to trace the softly curved rump of the zebra in front of him when he's ambushed by a trio of black fingerprints, stamped on the heart of that dazzling whiteness like a depraved wellspring. Day ruined. He puts his pencil down and looks desolately at his fingers, the tips dirty from touching the notes, a few lone crumbs stuck to the slightly sticky skin like forgotten mountain climbers on a pink slope. Then he rips the paper in one brutal movement, crosses his arms while falling to the ground, and buries himself in one of his gloomy, bad-tempered trances, which can last for hours, or days, and from which nobody knows how to rescue him.

How his father does it, he doesn't know, he'll never know. He certainly takes good care of his hands. He washes them frequently no matter where he is, but particularly at the office, and always with his own soap, which he keeps in the second drawer of his desk and takes into the bathroom with him, where he scrubs them furiously and joyfully; and he files his nails—including the cubist one, which he caught in the drawer of a steel file cabinet when he was a young boy, so that now it looks like a pitched roof, one side black, the other white with a hint of pink, split down the middle by a sharp white line—with a dedication that couldn't be further from his treatment of his toenails, which he surrenders to an unchecked growth that always ends up ruining his socks. But it can't be just that. It'd be easier to understand if he dealt in checks, promissory notes, credit cards, any of those sanitized substitutes for money that are beginning to come into use at the time, the task force of an arrogant, cutting-edge economy, which he sees members of his stepfamily already juggling familiarly, particularly his mother's husband, whose checkbook covers are tattooed with the same beautiful uppercase initials that appear on the haunches of the cattle grazing on his land to the south of the city. But his father is cash, a hundred percent. Of course, he's familiar with all the modern forms of payment, because of his work, and because he doesn't live in a cave, but he's very careful to use them and treat them with the same aristocratic disdain with which he condemns calculators and, a few decades later, when they wouldn't do him any harm, glasses, hearing aids, and walking sticks.

Always the wad of notes. No matter where he is, whether on the street or playing tennis, on a layover in Dakar airport or getting up from his TV chair—his true place in the world, in his final years—to fetch his perennial divorcé's dinner of roast chicken and potatoes, which he orders from the deli on the corner, he always seems to have his money within arm's reach. *All* of his money, which of course includes the pounds, Swiss francs, dollars, and lire with which he usually impresses the delivery boy, holding the wad right under his nose to select the notes he'll use to pay him. The question is how to tell, in light of this law of cash, the single, ironclad axiom that rules his economy from beginning to end, whether his father is rich or poor. It's a question that will never cease to confuse him. The size of the wad, its arrogant bulge, the variety of denominations and colors it comprises, even its organizing principle: all of this seems to be a sign of wealth, of the wealthiest of wealths, direct, immediate wealth, which doesn't need to be translated or converted or passed through an intermediary before it can be put to use. But whenever he catches his father taking the wad from a pocket to pay for something, anything, two cinema tickets, a pair of sneakers, a small tub of ice cream, twenty-eight nights at the Croatian hotel in Villa Gesell, which nevertheless are so sublime that to him they're priceless, and allows himself to marvel at the idea that this bundle of notes, which his father handles as masterfully as a cardsharp, as though he'd been born with it in his hand, is in fact all his money, there comes a moment when the spell stands still, as though lashed with a malevolent whip, and what appears after it's dispersed is its flip side of doubt and suspicion: the terror—arising precisely from the evidence that what he sees there is it, that there's nothing more—that it might run out, run out completely, with no chance of being replaced, once and for all.

But if he had any idea about anything, he'd understand that the amount doesn't matter. The fact that his father always has all his money to hand doesn't make him rich or poor. It makes him ready. It's simple: his father is prepared. He can do what he likes whenever he likes, buy what he likes, go where he likes. Rich or poor, he's free. The idea is too abstract—reckless, even—for a boy of six, which might explain its fate in his imagination: it spends years hibernating in a dark, remote limbo, along with other ideas that brush by him sometimes but never really reach him, as though they never quite believe him worthy of themselves, and so keep their distance, tempting him and contemplating him but remaining as far from his reach as any other wonder of the adult world, like shaving, for example, or knowing all the streets in a city. Until the day he finds out that Sartre—who's described as the ugliest philosopher in the world, according to the person who entrusts this fact to him—boasts that he carries everything he needs in order to survive in his coat pockets—money, obviously, but also tobacco; a notebook and something to write with; a penknife; a small, difficult book; and a spare pair of glasses—and the idea is reawakened and fills his head with a blinding clarity.

Free, yes, but free to do what? Probably to vanish into thin air from one day to the next, without giving any warning or leaving any clues, just as his mother—hoping to open his eyes once and for all, she says—tells him his father's father did: a true founder of the school of family escapology who, incapable even of coming up with a remotely original excuse, announces in his shirtsleeves one day that he's going to the corner to buy cigarettes and never comes back, only sending a sign of life two years later, from the hotel he's lording it over with a Spanish woman in a new, still unfinished resort on the Costa del Sol, one of those paradises for enterprising tourists where the sky, judging by the photo on the postcard that arrives at the house with no envelope, with the postmark stamped directly on the fugitive's handwriting and the unbearable indignity of its revelations on show, is a fluorescent cyan, and an army of palm trees guards the sunbathers while they lie on the sand.

He never gets to see this postcard, which like so many things is mislaid and then lost, or perhaps destroyed by his grandmother in a fit of spite, or maybe she takes it out of circulation and keeps it locked in some secret place so that, when everyone is asleep and the neighborhood is as calm as it was the day her husband left her, she can worship it in silence, with the tortured loyalty of a victim opening a secret altar to worship the tragedy that still sets her hopeless life alight. He never sees it, but he knows it perfectly from descriptions; not so much those he gets from his mother, who returns to the subject frequently, as if the famous postcard had cast the mold for all the later disasters, starting with her own divorce, but rather from his father, who's the first to mention it to him, and in the bitterest terms, and who thirty years later can evoke in lush detail the perfect beach day that shines on one side of the card, and remember precisely how many palm trees there are in each row, and how many sunbathers, and what colors their bathing suits are, how many floors have already been built in the apartment block growing across the promenade, how many clouds you can see, and how much the postmark says it cost to send this card from Torremolinos to Buenos Aires in 1956.

In fact, he comes across it thirty years later in a second-hand bookshop in the center of the city. He's been there for a while, getting his fingers mucky on the dusty spines of the books—perhaps the only objects capable of collecting more dirt than money. He's not looking for anything in particular, and this lack of purpose aggravates his disappointment in all these little books of poems, scrawny vanity publications, and colossal, idiotic novels with garish covers that nobody will ever buy, not him nor anybody else. Not holding out much hope, simply to entertain himself a little, he moves to the table opposite, which holds a series of large cardboard boxes containing a jumble of period newspapers, old magazines in plastic sheaths, film stills, sheets of stamps, and postcards. And while he looks at his blackened fingertips, which the layers of dust seem to have hardened, the bookseller, a burly asthmatic in ancient suspenders who's been walking around the shop putting more stock on the tables, stops beside him for a moment and drops a transparent envelope full of old postcards into the box his hands are sunk in. On top of the pile, balancing on one corner and staring straight at him, is the postcard of the beach in Torremolinos. He takes the envelope out of the box and shows it to the bookseller. He wants to buy it. The lot's being sold whole, or not at all. He asks how much and listens incredulously: it costs a hundred and twenty times what his fugitive grandfather paid to send the original postcard. He's willing to buy it even so, but when he puts his hand in his pocket, he realizes that he's not carrying that much money on him. He passes the envelope containing the postcards to the bookseller and asks him to put it aside, so that nobody can come along while he's gone and take a liking to it, and goes in search of an ATM. The closest one is out of service; there's a line at the second one; the third has run out of money. He wanders around for another fifteen minutes before coming up with the cash. By the time he gets back, the bookstore has closed. He rests his forehead on the glass, makes a visor with his hands, and spots the envelope on top of the cardboard box, lying with an air of disdainful superiority on an old copy of a political weekly—from back when the early years of the seventies were flying, or rather shooting, by—on whose cover a '73-model yacht designed by the Martinoli shipyard is being blown to pieces by twenty kilos of trotyl, while a police chief suspected of torturing political prisoners waits on board, ready to set off on his weekly outing to Tigre. The cyan blue of the Torremolinos sky dazzles even through the triple filter of the transparent envelope, the dirty glass of the shop's door, and the iron shutter-curtain. But the farther he gets from the bookstore, the hazier the details of the photo become. The half moon of the beach trembles and evaporates like a landscape seen in passing from a distance, and the colors of the bathing suits start to fade. How can he be sure that it was the one, that it was *the* postcard? His grandfather and his father, the only people who could confirm it, are dead. He never goes back to that bookshop.

No bank account; checks are unthinkable; pension, taxes—his father isn't made for all that. He has married and divorced, had cars and apartments, renewed his ID card, signed rental contracts, worked for companies, and signed business letters on letterhead. But he keeps his money in rolled-up socks and only applies for his tax ID number when he's over seventy-five years old, and even then reluctantly, after doing everything in his power to avoid it, before finally being convinced by a neighbor who lives two floors above him and offers to help him with the paperwork. He's a classic misfit, the type his father would blindly follow anywhere: he has only a few teeth left, calls himself a public accountant, and wanders around the block in old sweatpants, dragging along a pair of plastic sandals. He's a fanatical supporter of San Lorenzo, like his father, and an expert in numbers by vocation too, but he's also sufficiently artful with shady numbers to understand a basic principle that his father will never understand: that nobody can dedicate themselves to such numbers and give nothing to the law in exchange, and that the tax ID number is the most innocuous nothing that can be given. But when the accountant tells his father that the number has finally arrived, he doesn't go outside, bathe, or answer the phone for three days; he lies sprawled on his TV chair with his back turned to the machine, so depressed by the magnitude of his own lack of principle that he doesn't even have the energy to press the ON button on the remote. And nevertheless, when they find the lover of crostini dead at the bottom of the river, horribly swollen by the more than three days he's spent in the water, and without the attaché case that reportedly contains the bundle of dollars everyone wants to know about, the only person to bring up the subject of the money and, after performing some mental magic, estimate how much has been lost or stolen—whether from the bottom of the river when the helicopter is found or earlier, sometime between takeoff and the crash, nobody knows—is his father, his crackpot father, who never saw the dead man in person. As far as he knows, nobody in his stepfamily mentions it, though they're so closely linked to the dead man by friendship, by business, and by class interests that it's difficult to imagine them not knowing what role he played in the powder keg in Villa Constitución, what mission he was on when he boarded the helicopter that morning, and also, of course, how much money he had been given to achieve it.

But someone, one of them, must know something. Know, even though they won't tell—because, as he hears said more than once in the mansion in Mar del Plata, only those who don't have money talk about it: those who had it once and lost it, and those who made it through unpleasant means, which is to say those who made it at all, rather than inheriting it. Maybe the widow doesn't have much to say; she might have been kept in the dark by the logic of secrecy and the parallel worlds surrounding militant leaders' immediate families and the intimate circles of prominent businessmen at the time, ordinary people, wives, husbands, children, siblings, who find out who they've been sharing their homes with, their beds, their plans, their vacations, only when someone calls them and asks them to come to the morgue and identify the bodies. And meanwhile this same logic is beginning to rule everything, the specific and the general, the life of companies like the one that employed the dead man for so long and life throughout the whole country, with its Martinoli yachts flying through the air, its industrial belts in flames, and its cross-eyed economy, which has forked into one laughable official dimension, with an anemic, purportedly ruling currency, and another, the so-called black one, where the virus of the dollar releases its toxic fumes.

Yes, everything tends to the shady, the double, and what happens on one side of the mirror isn't necessarily known on the other, even when the repercussions might be felt there, might make an impact or even pose a danger. One winter's night at the Hotel Gloria, his father, taking more trouble than he has in the four preceding days of their vacation in Rio de Janeiro, hurries him into the shower, has his dinner brought up to the room, puts him to bed and tucks him in, and, after turning out every light but the one on the nightstand, tells him that tonight, also for the first time in four days, he's going out on his own, without him, and that it's very possible he'll be back late. When he gets back, he wants to find him asleep. And then, raising his voice a little, exaggerating the note of admonition until he's almost singing, he delivers a string of assorted warnings and pieces of advice, at times so varied—don't raid the minibar; don't use the bed as a trampoline; be careful of the flock of toucans that might suddenly invade the room, thirsty for revenge for the fake toucan food they gave them that afternoon at the *jardim botanico*, really a few crumbs of old nougat that he accidentally smuggled from Buenos Aires in the pocket of his pants—that he, covered up to his chin and still terrified by the prospect of staying behind on his own, can't help laughing. But why can't he go with him? Why can't they go out together, just like last night when they went to the juice bar on the *beira-mar*, the seafront, or the night before that, when they went to the cinema to see *O dolar furado*—he repeated the title loudly on the way out—the Portuguese-dubbed version of *Un dólar marcado*, the western starring Giulianno Gemma they've already seen together half a dozen times in Buenos Aires? "It's grown-up time," his father says, putting a hand just liberated in protest back under the sheet. "I have to see a friend." "Now? At night?" he asks. Though he could swear that he's only asking for information, a routine explanation, a faint but uncontrollable trembling in his lower lip tells him that the matter is more serious than that, that he might be about to cry. "It's a friend who owes me money," says his father. And he leans toward him, kisses his still-damp hair, and heads for the door, putting on his blue blazer as he walks. He sees him pause in the hallway by the door, where he takes one last look at himself in the mirror and, with two sharp tugs, rescues his shirt's white cuffs, which had gotten caught under the sleeves of his jacket. Then he opens a dresser drawer, takes out a dark package, studies it for a few seconds with his head bowed, puts it in a pocket, and leaves.

He listens to his steps, which are muffled by the carpet, growing more distant and then suddenly quickening into the cocky little trot he always breaks into at the top of a flight of stairs, and he closes his eyes in resignation. It takes him a long time to get to sleep. He lies still in the bed, just as his father left him, ignoring the temptations stalking the room's darkness, the TV, his comic books, the *garoto* chocolates in the minibar, and his collection of Brazilian cruzeiros, which he's been accumulating since the beginning of the trip from change they've been given, and which are due their first audit. He's scared that if he moves, something in his father's life—in the mysterious, dangerous life he's decided to lead without him, away from him—might change, or be endangered. This is the way he's lying, as rigid as a dead man, as the dead man who can still make his head ring with the crostini-crackling that tormented him for whole summers when he's laid out in his coffin eight years later, when sleep creeps up on him in the hotel's dense silence, after it's begun to grow light outside and the old, tattered exhausts of the first buses full of workers have started roaring two floors below. His father wakes him up, as usual, by ruffling his hair, hair that the pillow has straightened at will, according to the vagaries of sleep, and that's now electrified, shooting locks charged with static in every direction. "Up, sleepyhead, or we'll miss breakfast," he says, standing up and turning his back to him, and then emptying his pants' pockets onto the nightstand. He covers his eyes so that the light that bursts into the room doesn't blind him. Then, very carefully, he opens his fingers just a tiny bit and watches him as though spying through the cracks of a blind: except for the blazer, which is hanging on the back of a chair, he's wearing the same clothes he had on when he went out last night.

This scene is replayed three times, identically, over the course of the trip, but the cloud of mysteries it brings with it pursues him for years. He can never understand how his father can call someone who owes him money a "friend." It's not the notion of debtors that he finds problematic; in fact, that's not new to him. How many times has he heard his father shout that people owe him money? Everyone owes him money, all the time. It's as though the world were split in two: his father, alone, and the huge wave of debtors that persecutes him. What he can't understand is why he declares it the way he does. There's an element of complaint in it (as though the money he's owed is a curse that can only be cast by yelling), but also a certain disconcerting pride that transforms the status of creditor into a privilege, a miraculous gift of the type that fate bestows on the heroes of apocalyptic films, like being fertile in a world sterilized by nuclear radiation, or the ability to speak or think on a planet populated by beasts. It's really the money itself that he finds disturbing. He can never imagine friendship and money coexisting without feeling scandalized. It's as though, by dint of some extraordinary cosmic misalignment, two radically foreign kingdoms have come together in an unknown territory, and it's anybody's guess what sort of unwonted plants and creatures will result. And since it's impossible for him to grasp, he naturally starts to jump to conclusions.

His father said "a friend" to ease his mind, to alleviate the worrying effect of "owes me money," the only charged and therefore true part of the sentence. But how can "a friend" share any reasonable sequence of events with the dark package that his father takes out of the drawer and puts in his pocket each of the three nights he goes out alone, leaving him in the eye of a storm of omens from which only sleep can free him? If "a friend" can't share a phrase with "owes money," what kind of phrase would it take to unabashedly unite "a friend" and "a revolver"? Because that's what his father takes with him every time he goes to see the friend who owes him money, a revolver, an 1873 Colt Peacemaker six-shooter with a walnut handle, just like the one Montgomery Wood, the hero of *O dolar furado*, uses when he tries to avenge his brother's murder. Which means his father is in danger. How did he not think of it earlier? That's obviously why he goes out alone. He leaves the Hotel Gloria, travels the length of the city in a taxi—one of the demented race cars that serve as taxis in Rio de Janeiro—and, with his Colt 1873 at the ready, tiptoes into a gloomy, unfamiliar apartment where everything from the arrangement of the furniture to the location of every last light switch and bell, everything that could either serve his purpose or hinder it, is obedient to someone else's will: that of the friend who owes him money. Which is to say his worst enemy, who won't only not return his money but will make the most of his local advantage, will surprise him, split his head open with the sharp edge of a rock or a trophy, and leave him sprawled on the floor, drowning in his own blood. Sometimes, years later—long after the enigma has been solved, when there's no longer anything to fear—he replays the scene to himself, more out of the peculiar inertia of internal fictions than anything else, and he's flooded with a very potent retrospective terror that can change the past instantaneously, at the lightest of brushes, and he lies awake for hours, his eyes wide open, until, when he's as exhausted as he was at eleven years old, he hears the frenzied cawing of the birds breaking the morning silence.

How much money can his father be owed? What sum could justify the ritual of those three sadistic nights: his being put to bed—almost like being locked away in a basement—and condemned to the nightmare of insomnia; his father spritzing himself with cologne and dressing and styling his hair so carefully; the revolver being put in his pocket. To say nothing of everything else, all of it as ominous and misshapen as a series of expressionist photograms: the taxi, the city in darkness, the apartment, the head split open by the corner of the trophy, the puddle of blood. How much more money than the dead man was carrying in the helicopter? How much less? The same amount? (In his mind, and this is an illness he won't be cured of until much later, and even then only by chance, any unknown quantity of money is by definition the same sum.) Three times this scene is replayed, and three times his father gives the same answer when, at the breakfast table the next morning, he gathers his courage and takes advantage of the state of idiotic beatitude his father sinks into on seeing the encyclopedic variety of fruits on offer at the hotel to ask him the question that has been macerating in his terrified imagination for, what, ten, twelve hours? Whether he finally got the money his friend owed him. All three times, the same answer: No. All three times, the same explanation: He couldn't find him. He went to his house, he rang the bell, nobody answered.

This answer seems possible, logical. That could happen, he thinks, while his little right hand—which is very skilled at drawing and sculpting monsters out of modeling clay and other such feats of dexterity, but astonishingly clumsy when it comes to more basic practical matters—struggles to spread butter on a long, vaguely oval slice of pumpernickel that looks like the sole of one of his shoes. But the third time he hears it, he freezes, stunned, with the piece of bread suspended midway between the plate and his mouth. What did he say? What's he talking about? It's not the fact that he's being lied to that shocks him. It's the wild disproportion he senses between the answer—which, incidentally, his father gives without even thinking about it, totally unfazed, while his hands pile up slices of *abacaxí* on his plate and his eyes flit eagerly to the platters of mango, papaya, guava, passion fruit, fruits that drive him crazy, as he often says in Buenos Aires, where they're nowhere to be found, but whose names he can't remember, and never will be able to—and the three nights of torment he's been made to endure. Something inside him darkens, as when a cloud drags its long, slow shadow across a scorched terrace. He no longer thinks of his father as a nocturnal adventurer who distracts night watchmen, forces windows, and slips, armed, into other people's houses to reclaim what is his at the risk of violent retaliation and even death. What if he's a coward? He considers the possibility for a second, and the image that had filled him with happiness earlier, when he woke up and almost crashed into it—his father by his side, safe and sound and acting as though nothing had ever happened, sitting on the edge of his bed in the early morning to recruit him for a breakfast orgy of fruit—becomes a proof of disgrace. He survived, which means he didn't have the courage to see it all the way through. He goes out, stops the taxi, gives the address, but when the taxi driver repeats it, loudly, the alarmed tremor in his voice makes him hesitate. The neighborhood's dark streets frighten him. He sees a light on in one of the apartment's windows and worries that his debtor friend is not alone. He arrives just as the other guy is coming out, and realizes that he didn't remember him being so tall, so stocky, so ready for anything.

The more he thinks about it, the surer he is that he's been tricked. But by now, after three nights of lying awake until dawn with his heart in his mouth, thinking he's been left fatherless in a hotel room in Rio de Janeiro, what apart from the scene he fears most could possibly satisfy him? This is how the imagination operates: by submitting its guinea pigs to extreme challenges of its own invention and recognizing their heroism only when they succumb, never when they survive. It's also how the period operates: those who make it back from the dead come back because they're cowards, because they've sold out or paid up, because they've struck a deal with the enemy, never because they've overpowered it. Not the dead crostini lover: at least he goes all the way down and doesn't come back. His father came back; he lives to tell the tale, as they say. But what type of tale would he have to tell to repay the torment he's made him suffer? Certainly not the string of abstractions he throws out when, and only when, it occurs to him to interrogate him during the remainder of the vacation. Never a single detail. The streets don't have names, the neighborhoods are "there," "on the other side of the *lagoa*," "before you reach the bridge." Nothing happens at a precise time. All the recurring events—the taxi, the house, the friend who never answers the intercom—are vague and insipid, like an illustration of a phrase in a foreign grammar book. Occasionally he thinks he's uncovered an unexpected nuance, a change in his father's tone of voice, some new piece of information that casts doubt on an earlier version of the facts: the neighborhood isn't that far away, he lets his taxi go when he gets there (when earlier he had preferred to make it wait), a lit-up balcony with plants appears where earlier there had only been the black square of a window. What type of plants? Ficus? Ferns? Dwarf palms? What emerges here is never the truth. It is, rather, the impression that anything that comes out of his father's mouth is and always will be a lie.

And another thing, though this occurs to him only later, when he's already back in Buenos Aires: If he never finds the friend who owes him money, why doesn't he come back to the hotel? Where does he spend the rest of those three nights? "At the casino, my darling," his mother says. Or rather releases amid the musical laugh she lets out after hearing his account of those three dismal nights at the Gloria, in particular at the phrase he quotes directly, as if his father were speaking through him—*A friend owes me money*—which she finds irresistibly comic. At first he doesn't intend to tell her about it. He is eleven years old. He has spent eight of those years—since the day his father, freshly bathed, as he always is for the decisive moments in his life, filled a bag with his white monogrammed shirts, his sports magazines, his cufflinks, his bottle of lavender water, his packet of imported cigarettes, his suede buckled shoes, and his shaving brush, and left the apartment on Ortega y Gasset forever—avoiding the role of double agent. He knows too well the explosive potential that certain pieces of information acquire when they pass from one camp to another. But then maybe that's exactly why he tells. Maybe when he gets back, tanner than he's ever been before or ever will be again, and sees his mother emptying his suitcase, and a little *carioca* sand falls out of a sock and trickles onto the carpet, maybe at that moment he realizes how much bitterness he has stored up. Casino? He stands staring at his mother in wary astonishment, like a con artist looking at a more skillful rival.

His father dies and not once in almost fifty years has he seen him gambling. Crying, yes, and being humiliated, and punching through the cheap wood of a hotel room's closet door, and secretly doing all manner of pathetic things, and standing with his hands on his hips, wearing an air of absolute perplexity, to examine the Fiat 600's engine as it smokes on the shoulder, and putting a piece of toilet paper on a shaving cut to stop it from bleeding, and lying to hide his shame, and furiously rubbing the first age spot to appear on the back of one of his hands. But that scene—the scene of his father sitting at a card table with a glass of whiskey, a cigarette smoking while it lies in a notch on the ashtray, one hand palm down and motionless on the green cloth, the other holding three poker cards in a fan at forty-five degrees, also facedown—will always be denied him. And his father will be the one who denies it, though he's open in everything, shameless even in matters of bodily intimacy, such as taking a bath or defecating—both of which he always does with the bathroom door open—or farting—one of his hobbies, in which he takes no heed of spatial limitations or social restrictions, and which he practices and teaches as devotedly as a crusader—but rigidly reserved when it comes to gambling. He can talk about it, share anecdotes about the casinos he frequents and the gamblers he knows, admit how much he won on his best night and how much he lost on his worst, and even manage to make the figures sound convincing. But his father never allows anybody to see him gambling. Nobody, least of all his loved ones, not even those who haven't the slightest objection to it—namely him, who as soon as he finds out that he gambles stops disdaining him as a coward and, though he knows he's deluded, starts to respect him again, to adore him, to envy the intimacy of this new world he's just discovered he reigns over. He doesn't want anybody near him when he gambles—period. Neither nearby nor hoping to emulate him. This is the source of the indolence that floods him— his father, who in any of his other strong suits, numbers, of course, and reading between the lines of newspapers, tennis, sports in general, predicting the success or failure of a play, is a born pedagogue if not an outright evangelist, a man who will not rest until he's emptied himself of everything he has to teach—whenever someone, usually him, begs him to impart a little of his great knowledge, like how to assume a poker face, ruses for winning at roulette, ways of dissembling, shuffling and dealing techniques, the stance to adopt in casinos, which drinks to order, how to pick out rivals with better cards than yours, how to talk to the person throwing the ball at a roulette wheel so that the right numbers come up. Once more, it's all vague and general or already common knowledge. The cloth is green; you drink whiskey, neat or with ice; it's a good idea to give a chip or two to the staff when a ball lands in your favor, and also to play at more than one table at a time; knowing how to lie is crucial. In other words, nothing. He can't decide whether his father refuses to share his knowledge so as not to cement his reputation as a gambler, out of shame—like a victim of some moral disease who believes that passing on what he has learned since catching it will pass on the disease itself—or because he's scared that if he shares it, his knowledge will take root in another gambler, a conscientious apprentice who, when chance brings them together at a card table someday, will clean up using the very techniques that he taught him. In any case, he will have to content himself with the version of his private gift that his father is prepared to share in public, which remains as opaque, as scandalously far from its original as the mercilessly mutilated versions of certain films that circulate under the censorship of the day: a sly, inconsequential bluff in a game of *truco* among friends, a rapid sleight with the dice cup at the beach club that gets him five of a kind, the whist tournaments played in the club's game room, in the middle of the day, while children play between the tables and old people nod off in groups, for a cash prize that, if he wins it—which according to his reputation at the club he does two out of every three times—is not enough to pay for the coffees he's drunk while competing.

It's the same for his mother. Recently married, with him already on the way, the unplanned fruit of one of the skirmishes they get entwined in before they've thought about whether they're in love, though they're both already equally fixated on the idea of getting away from their respective families as soon as possible, she notices that her perfect stomach, which is as flat as a board and blessed with the kind of skin people dream of—one of those stomachs that always appears in black and white and extreme close-up in the artistic photography of the day, looking like a beach or a lunar landscape—is stretching and beginning to bulge as steadily as her husband's nightly returns to the apartment on Ortega y Gasset grow later. The night she realizes, the telephone is silent, the cleaner at the office tells her that everyone has left, the meal is cold and already inedible, the cinema plans aborted. One night he doesn't show up until twenty past four in the morning. When he appears, with a long day's stubble and a halo of cigarette smoke strong enough to knock her flat, he says he got into an accident in the street: he left the office and was crossing the street when some idiot drove right over him. He didn't get out of the police station at Suipacha and Arenales until half an hour ago. She doesn't know what to think. She doesn't know him. She only knows about him, and about the clumsy but comforting force of his Germanic lunges, about everything in him that exasperates and disappoints her, about the collection of flaws that define him, and everything that she will dedicate herself to criticizing for the forty years she spends without him, free of him. She can picture the altercation in the street, although she knows from experience that if it really happened, it wasn't because of an abuse of his pedestrian's right of way, unless by right of way her husband understands what he obviously does understand—the right to cross the road when and where he likes, preferably wherever the traffic is densest, when the cars have a green light and no pedestrian with half a brain would think to cross, let alone as defiantly and arrogantly as a true artist of danger.

She thinks he has a lover. His mother is young and beautiful; she's as voracious as every woman on the run and has the rancor of an aristocratic lady in exile, forced to dress in secondhand clothes and eat reheated food. The ideal candidate to be tied down with a child by the first scoundrel to seduce her while he swans around elsewhere. It happens to all of them. Why should she be the exception? His mother never even mentions it. Every time she feels the urge to ask, she has the sensation of treading on very fragile ground, like a carpet made of glass. It's as though she'd been born without skin. She's frightened by her clothes every time they brush against her, of the noise her throat makes when she swallows, and of the tremulous half-moons of light that the sun projects onto the ceiling when it breaks through the crown of the banana palm whose branches overrun the balcony. Some mornings she wakes up and doesn't even have the courage to open her eyes. But the thing that terrifies her most is giving him a reason to get rid of her—and she thinks anything could be a reason. One night she goes to bed alone. Every minute she passes without him is a minute lost in the torture of waiting for him, sinks her a meter further into a dark morass that won't kill her but does poison her with hatred. At ten past six in the morning, she hears a key scratching at the door. She shifts onto her side in the bed, turning her back to him, and pretends to sleep. She doesn't want to speak to him, doesn't want to see him. Only to *sense* him, as though she were hidden behind a door with a knife under her clothes, waiting for the perfect moment to sink it into his chest. He doesn't make any pretenses. He doesn't even try to be quiet so as not to wake her. He takes off his clothes—a cufflink jangles against the bronze base of the bedside lamp—showers with the door open, gets dressed, goes out again. She doesn't go back to sleep. She will never forget the sound of those keys.

In the middle of the morning, her mother comes to visit. She brings new clothes for the baby, another of the ensembles covered in belts, ruffles, and bows that she buys compulsively, enchanted by the idea—an accurate one, incidentally, which makes it even more depressing to her daughter—that they're just like the clothes they bought for her before she was born, and she accepts them and files them away in the closet where she keeps the still lifes, swans made of green glass, and cretonne curtains that have been lavished upon her since she got married. After thirty sleepless hours, she can't even stir a cup of tea, let alone hold one, and the cup smashes to pieces on the kitchen floor. She starts to cry and confesses, and as soon as she has confessed she realizes her mistake. If there are two people in the world who cannot help her, they are her parents. Her mother is a tiny, bitter woman, who believes she's given all she had to give—as little as that may have been—and who now limits herself to relaying her daughter's dramas to her husband. Her father, a corpulent despot who communicates in growls and wears very high-waisted pants, receives the problems and bends them to his own will, using them to support the cause he will never tire of championing: demonstrating to his daughter that, for as long as she chooses to live away from them, her life will be a catastrophe. She pleads with her mother not to say anything, not to humiliate her in front of her father. Her mother, smiling at her, tells her not to worry. But it's too late. The moment she gets home, the woman picks up the telephone, calls the factory, and passes her report on to her husband.

There's a young man from Tucumán at the factory, the brother of a foreman recently fired for stealing, whom his grandfather kept on partly out of spite, to torment the man he'd fired—from whose betrayal he never recovers, being an immigrants'-son-turned-boss and an incorrigible paternalist—and partly because it's convenient. The boy is naïve; for a few coins he'll do things that nobody else would do— errands, preparing *mate cocido*, acting as a chauffeur or night guard—and he has ambitions that his gratitude to the boss only strengthens. He's enlisted for some overtime (yet more to add to the great quantity he's already amassed, which even combined would never add up to a wage): to see what the boss's son-in-law is up to. Six hundred of the pesos of the day, pesos moneda nacional: exactly the amount his father needs, four nights later, to stay in at a surprisingly, inexplicably adverse poker table, which something tells him it's still not time to leave even though he's been completely cleaned out. It's five past five on a raw winter's dawn, and his father's gone out into the street to smoke in his shirtsleeves. A sweater would keep him warm. Gambling is better: it makes him invincible. He stubs his cigarette out on a paving stone, spits a resigned stream of smoke into the frozen air, the last of the night, and when he raises his eyes he catches a glimpse of the boy from Tucumán's shadow moving across the street, or rather shivering from the cold in the alley he's been standing guard in for some time. It takes him five seconds to work out that it's *someone*, ten to cross the street, twenty to catch up with the boy from Tucumán after he tries to run away, half a minute to recognize him—he remembers him well: he's the boy who laughed under his breath on one of the two visits his father has paid to the factory in order to please his father-in-law, when he said that his favorite thing about the place was the workers' clothes—and a minute—prolonged by the bottle truck that drives past, making a racket that obliges him to repeat the arrangement he's proposing a second time—to take from him the six hundred pesos he's just earned. It's only a loan, he tells him, underpinning the idea with subtle nepotistic insinuations. He'll return it in two hours, without fail, in this same alleyway, only quadrupled. A little while later, she emerges from another strenuous bout of insomnia and finds him in the kitchen, sitting with the back of a chair between his legs, swirling a recently made cup of coffee in his hands. He's just shaved, he looks younger than ever, and he smiles like an awestruck child. "I was dead. A real beating: I hadn't won a single hand," he tells her, his eyes wide. "The guy from Tucumán your father hired to follow me ended up rescuing me."

Gambling is his thing—just as other men might take drugs, shoplift, cross-dress, or drive at 200 kilometers per hour—and he's alone in it, and everything that will ever be known of him while he's in his thing until they both die off will only emerge by error or accident. Because "things" are worlds, and no world can close itself off completely, no matter how perfect it is. That morning, in the kitchen, his mother realizes that there will never be space in him for her. It has nothing to do with her, with what she does or does not do. The proof is his absolute lack of guilt, the almost jovial ease with which he skips over the trouble of a confession and assumes something that for her, until that moment, had been a mystery, and had tortured her unbearably. He's never mentioned his gambling before for precisely the reason that he's talking about it now, which is also why he's talking about it in the way he is, like someone thinking aloud, without any need for interlocutors. His silence has never been a secret. That's why he never felt the urge to confess. For his mother, this is the first and perhaps the only night of gambling, and it's charged with surprises and revelations. For his father, it's one more in a series. That's why he's talking about it as though his mother had known all about each of those other ones that led up to it.

And now he knows, too. He's almost more aware of it than his father himself, given the mimetic impulse awoken in him by certain indeterminately sick people, the undiagnosed or those trapped in the webs of confusing diagnoses (melancholics, perverts, dreamers, idolaters, procrastinators), with whose ills he claims both a rare intimacy, as though he had suffered them in some other life, and a peculiar distance, characterized by compassion and astuteness and more befitting a doctor than a patient. "At the casino, my darling," his mother tells him after bursting out laughing, and once the first moment of astonishment has passed, he peeps around the door she's cracked open for him and sees a rapid panorama of it all, the gold and red of the carpets, the flashing lights on the slot machines, the waiters carrying trays of drinks between tables, the employees in bow ties and waistcoats taking piles of chips out of boxes, the tables surrounded by gamblers on their feet, the baize tabletops, the cards coming out of the *sabot*, and, with his back to him, his jacket off and hanging from the back of his seat, two halos of sweat around his armpits, and his head enveloped in the smoke from his own cigarette, his father, leaning very far forward, his shoulders sunken and his elbows resting on the edge of the table.

Sometimes he can't help himself, and he lets slip a question about roulette wheels, croupiers, cheats, or the secret, silent rooms where he imagines big winners go to exchange their chips for money. Other times he skips straight to action, thinking he's much more likely to rouse his father by making himself an example and demonstrating everything he doesn't know and wants to learn. And so he finds any reason to start shuffling cards, and shuffles badly, exaggerating his clumsiness, trying to stir his father's pride and convince him to teach him, or deliberately loses card games in an attempt to awaken his pity or his fury and so finally extract the drops of his expertise that will save him from more humiliation. They're feeble, hopeless efforts. His father responds indifferently, with evasions that he accepts without protest. After a while he stops trying. Lost cause. But how he rejoices in those moments when something unexpected, a random, utterly unintentional spur, dents the shield protecting his father and his world and reopens for a second the door his mother once opened; when a tiny but dazzling flash of that forbidden realm escapes and reaches him, like music escaping a party and reaching some far-off room, and he feels as though a seed is being planted in him. It happens rarely, generally with movies, TV programs, plays, books that at some point touch on the subject of gambling, gamblers, the practice of betting. Everything will be fine, the scenes will be flowing as normal, the film more or less entertaining, the book well or poorly written, the play moving forward—until someone shows up and cuts a deck of cards, or a character tells a story about a night at a casino while sitting at the table after dinner,

ALAN PAULS

or a ball takes a few hesitant leaps on the slope of a spinning roulette wheel, and his father, who had been following
the developments in silence, entrenched in his indifference,
suddenly stiffens, as if struck by an invisible dart, and all of
his senses, which until that moment have been floating and
dispersed, surface again on his face as though called up for
battle, and then fire on what he's been looking at. In a fraction
of a second, he's transformed into what he's always been but
had been keeping in reserve: the defender of an experience
that nobody else knows firsthand, and about which only he
possesses the ultimate truth. Being a film fanatic, for example,
he readily defends the liberties taken by cinema in the name
of art as instances of poetic license that no demand from reality can ever rightfully challenge, and yet he's feverishly
sensitive when it comes to films about gambling. Everything
strikes him as sloppy and ludicrous, not because it's artifi-
cial but because it's wrong. His arguments, when he makes
them—when he doesn't restrict himself to giving a sarcastic
little smile instead, a gesture of disdain he aims at the television, the scene, the screen where the outrage is being committed—are unspecific, always general, often sententious.
They're really vetos, laws that can only be formulated nega-
tively. "Nobody who's ever played baccarat looks at women
while he's playing," he says. Or: "For a true gambler, cash is
never a problem." Or: "Gamblers don't have lucky rituals."
Or: "There's no such thing as a nice croupier." Or: "No gambler wins or loses everything in the first hour of play." Or:
"Nobody ever plays everything." He's also riled by the over-
all aesthetic effect, the gleaming, almost glossy image with
which cinema beautifies gambling, where the backs of the
playing cards twinkle like mirrors and the ice in the glasses
like diamonds, the green baize looks like English grass, and
the good gamblers are always elegant while the bad ones
are monsters covered in scars and given to the vilest tricks,

incapable of doing or deciding anything without the help of the entourage of baleful assistants monitoring the table incognito. But the heart of the reproach is something else, something more fundamental, more radical. What sickens his father is that they're always secondhand versions, hearsay, pale echoes of echoes. They might keep audiences pinned to their seats, smash the box office, and claim to be based on true stories, but to his father—to anyone who's been submerged in the original experience—it's obvious that nobody involved in the concoction of these swindles has ever been there. None of them has lived the gambling life. And it's this lack of life that poisons these representations with an irremediable falseness.

Maybe this is his father's real life, this hidden one, the one they never see, this strange combination of gated paradise and toxic cellar, of orgiastic oasis and forced-labor camp, of which all they can ever hope to know comes from the leaks his father allows to escape every so often, almost against his will, like a medium opening his mouth and speaking and closing it again only when instructed to by the spirit speaking through him. It's a slightly distressing idea: it forces him to think of the father he can see, first the everyday one (while he's still married to his mother), then the weekend one (after the order to leave Ortega y Gasset), as a sort of body double for some invisible other, a replica that mechanically, as though following an instruction manual, carries out everything that should be done by one father, the original one, who is apparently too busy guessing cards, doubling bets, and frightening rivals with hands he doesn't have to do a father's work.

Eventually, though, he ends up getting used to it. Gambling is a world, and it works. It has its own rules, schedules, customs, uniforms, backdrops, props. Like every world—no matter what dangers it contains—its founding principle is that it's habitable. It might be distressing, but he now knows, or can guess, where his father is when he doesn't find him where he hopes to find him, where he and maybe his mother before him most need him, sitting by his side in the middle of the night when he has one of the nightmares that take hold of him without waking him up and make him sit up very straight in his bed, like Pinocchio, his eyes open and as unseeing as coins, or calling the pediatrician after taking the thermometer out of his armpit, or cleaning the bits between his toes. It's much worse, really, to imagine him crossing Rio de Janeiro at night in a brightly colored Volkswagen Beetle flying at the speed of light in search of a nameless, faceless debtor who no doubt couldn't have anything further from his mind than paying the debt he's about to be reminded of.

Besides, it's been clear since very early on, since before he could think for himself, as they say, that if there's anyone who can determine where life is, it's his father. In fact, he makes himself the authority on its everyday allocation (though his own existence demonstrates, perhaps in spite of itself, that there's nothing less certain or less obvious than the things we take for granted when we talk about life) and, like a surveyor, traces the frontiers—or rather reveals the invisible ones that were always there—between simulations of life and real life, shams and experiences, disguises and the naked truth. Even when he was a young boy, accompanying his father on his rounds through the business district was like taking a crash course in the art of appraising other people's lives. (Although "appraising" carries a trace of optimism: his father is a brutal evaluator, for whom nuances are pure affectation or gradations of fear. For him, there are two options: you're either alive, or you're dead.) You can start anytime. At the office, for example. He's come straight from school to see him; they're about to go out for lunch. The first lesson (like almost all of them) is conducted on the move, subtly imparted while they cross the office diagonally on the way to the elevator, fully exposed—particularly him, with his shyness, his bangs, and his pants' knee patches torn by the schoolyard's rough paving: an exotic animal, like all creatures from the outside who end up in the world of work—to the scrutiny of the other employees. While he walks and gives out general greetings, nodding his head and smiling, his father lets him in on the death certificates he's already signed: "The fat woman with the hairband: dead. The guy typing with two fingers: dead. That one selling coffee: dead. That ugly woman who talks to you like you're three years old: dead, dead, dead." The sequence shot follows them into the elevator that jolts them downstairs, taking in the operator, who's practically asleep (dead), through the lobby, with the doorman who's shuffling envelopes with greasy fingers (dead), into the street, with the redheaded guy selling candy at a kiosk (dead), the woman selling flowers (dead), and the newsstand owner closing his stand to go eat (dead). All dead. This is essentially the whole lesson. Dead: which is to say—according to the variety of existentialism prevailing in the region at the time, a civil servants' kind of existentialism, with the expert on accountants' woes Mario Benedetti in the role of Albert Camus, his novel *The Truce* in that of *The Rebel*, and his own father in that of official spokesperson for the dogma—perpetual hostages in the cells of a wretched, obligatory, monochrome life (gray being the color of *horror vacui*, according to the palette of the era) that offers no surprises nor any prospect of change. As time goes by, he thinks he comes to understand that life—which seems so universal, so evenly distributed—is actually a rare good that shows up where he would not at first have expected to find it: in children, beggars, stray dogs, crazy people—the only ones, according to his father, who meet the sole condition that makes life real: having the nerve to challenge everything. The barefoot boy putting a dirty hand through the window of a car stopped at a light; the beggar howling in an alley, covered in bags of trash; the puppy boldly sniffing the vulva of an arrogant Afghan hound; the madman and his private world of burning souls and organs consuming one another: these are the few happy anomalies his father seems to recognize in this general theater of the dead. There's more life there, he says, in that human wilderness, in those bodies covered in calluses, scabs, scars, than anywhere else.

He agrees in silence, because at a certain age any more or less self-assured show of authority is met with agreement. Even so, he would like to learn, to know where his father got his skill for tracing the dividing line, which signs to look out for and how to read them in order to decide what is genuine, free, sovereign life, and what is the parody that attempts to usurp it. Even at this age, he likes solid reasoning. He can admire the edge of a decision, or the timely impact of a bombshell, but what captivates him about both is also what frightens him: how sudden they are, and how soon they're over. Besides, if the taxi driver who spends his whole life cursing the other cars on the road is dead, as dead as the cashier who serves them at the bank, who spends hours counting other people's money without even lifting her head, and as the waitress in the phony Italian restaurant where they usually have lunch, who's red with embarrassment at the prostitute's uniform she's made to wear, a shirt undone to her belly button and a tight skirt that hardly covers her buttocks—if all these people who for better or worse breathe, peel open their eyelids every morning, and feel the icy thrusting of water at their gums, and are scared, and speak to other people are dead, oh so dead, as his father says of the ugly woman at the office who waves a useless hand in the air to ingratiate herself to him from a distance, and generally of more extreme cases, those that no earthquake or revolution could resuscitate, what about that close family friend of his mother's husband, who leaves behind a widow and two orphans, also leaving his mother's husband in a state of shock, dreaming about his body at the bottom of the river for months, until he feels as though he can't breathe and wakes up, his heart having almost stopped beating, pressing his pillow into his face with his own hands.

He's his first dead person. Like all first dead people, he has the rare quality of being simultaneously implausible and inevitable. The moment he arrives in the overheated room where the wake's being held, everything—the whispering, the soft light coming from the lamps on the floor and the tables, the furtive sound of every movement, the uniform color of the clothing, the air of monotony enveloping everything— prepares him to come face-to-face with a dead person, forces him to believe in it, to accept without a shadow of a doubt the evidence that he is dead. But when he gets to the coffin and sees the corpse all made up and dressed as if it's going out for the night, the first thing that crosses his mind is a remark too shameful to say aloud: "Okay, that's enough. Let's put an end to this farce. You can get up now." The truth of a lifeless body lacks nothing. It's irreducible, as hard as stone. But it's precisely this kind of impassive superciliousness that demands all the surrounding spectacle, the zealous care and beautification that turn every dead body into a strange mixture of puppet, waxwork, and actor. Even so, for all their artificiality, our first dead bodies are like a note struck by a pianist before he begins to play, which melts away no sooner than it has been heard but lingers throughout the whole piece as a key, guiding and making sense of it; they radically and permanently alter the world as we know it, injecting it with the sole possibility—the possibility of elimination—that was unimaginable to us the second before we came face-to-face with that corpse, because it was the opposite of the world itself.

And in this case, there's also the matter of the money. Where is life—his father's old question, which the dead man makes flesh, exposing it to the fragility and menace that color the world after every brush with misfortune—often gets mixed up with the other question, where is the money, which snakes through the wake in an undertone (in the way that vulgar, malicious, or funny conversation sometimes circulates in solemn and serious situations, deliberately disturbing the solemnity in order to make it more bearable, or maybe to remind us what cheap stuff it's made of) and sparks a few deliberations when a guest appears who should theoretically be able to answer the question, someone high up at the iron-and-steel company, a police official, the two or three army and navy officers who arrive in uniform, preceded by a compact phalanx of guards, and who restrict themselves to squeezing the hands of anyone who approaches them as soon as they see them coming, as though they were the chief mourners—though they never met the dead man in person and they're quick to leave as soon as they've stood at attention next to the coffin—and not the people who have been there for hours, wasting away in the sickly light of that apartment. Where. Where is the money.

They won't be the ones to tell, if they even know the answer. There's nothing to make them. The only person who could do that is the dead man, who might have found out before everybody else, when he goes up to the roof of the iron-and-steel company's Buenos Aires headquarters, boards the helicopter sitting there with its blades spinning, sits down, and signals to his assistant to give him the attaché case containing the money, only to discover that the assistant is empty-handed and now closing the helicopter door with a slam and telling the pilot to take off. They were relying on him. He's remained loyal to the company's interests for how many years? Twenty? How many times has he saved them from using forceful measures? How many union leaders has he shut up? He's the ideal man for this undertaking, the only one capable of understanding its exceptional nature, a nature that calls for emergency operating procedures justified by an equally exceptional situation that's raging out of control. Nobody ever imagined that he would oppose out of principle, or that he even had his own principles independent of the company's. But when the time comes, he objects to all of it: the means, the end, the very idea. His loyalty remains intact, but there are certain lines he is not willing to cross. It comes as a surprise. The real problem, which there's no fixing, is that it also comes too late. It becomes clear not only that he won't do it, but also that he knows too much. If it comes down to a loyal soldier with moral sensitivities and a perfect plan that will pacify the whole region and that comes with the government's blessing, which are they likely to choose?

The money must be there. Not twelve hours after the family announces that the helicopter hasn't arrived at its destination, a procession of vehicles a kilometer and a half long brings local police, federal agents sent from the capital, and a squad of select union thugs, in total some four thousand men in 105 vehicles (including private cars with no license plates, patrol cars, and assault cars), armed with long guns and kitted out with the accessories of intimidation that will inspire frenzy throughout the country for the next eight years—fake Ray-Bans, hoods, peaked caps, green or navy-blue berets—to Villa Constitución, the city once named the capital of the red belt of the Paraná River, to do away with a troublesome trade union group and uproot a subversive plot against the nation's heavy industry—a task that from that moment on they'll pursue almost unchecked, paid alternately by the chief of staff and the head of labor relations at the iron-and-steel company to the tune of a hundred and sometimes a hundred and fifty dollars each a day, and enjoying the use of the plant's helipad for the police helicopters, the parking lots for their cars, the plant's dining rooms for affordable lunches and dinners, the comfortable houses, originally meant for executives, for sleeping, watching television, and playing cards, and the workers' lodgings for interrogations and torture and stockpiling the loot from their daily raids.

The money is there, but it can't be seen, and he soon realizes that this is almost always the case. Maybe disappearing isn't an unpleasant accident, one of many eventualities eagerly awaiting money, but actually its very logic, a fatal tendency it has. Maybe, he thinks, that's the main similarity between money and life—more so even than the reproductive impulse, which they also share. It's there, but it's always embodied in or translated into something else: clothes, magazines, food, buildings, machines, school supplies, records, cinema tickets, thugs in dark glasses who stick their forearms out the window while they cock their Czechoslovakian guns. This is why he's glad that his father prefers not to pretend and always walks around with his pockets full of banknotes: because he likes the anachronistic challenge this represents. He trusts only what he sees, and what he sees, what circumstances dictate that his father sees—just as others before him saw grains of salt, seashells, feathers, or gold—is printed paper.

One day not long after the afternoon when he sees his first dead person—a day on which his mother, with a certain gravity in her voice, arranges a formal meeting with him, saying she wants to "talk to him about something," even though they live in the same house—he starts to wonder whether the compensation the crostini lover's widow received from the iron-and-steel company—as exceptional and possibly as ample a consignment as that which should have been on board the helicopter and which in a way condemned the dead man to death, since it's used to pay for the troops who are meanwhile turning mattresses over, stealing wedding rings, and ripping off testicles in Villa Constitución—is paid in cash. He's wondering this at the exact moment his mother appears in the living room, freshly showered, with her head wrapped in one of the towel turbans that suit her so well, and hands him an envelope containing two typed pages, which she asks him to read and sign at the bottom.

It takes him a little while to understand what it is he's reading. "In the event of an accident ..." "compensation ..." "as a result of which ..." "through the stipulated premium." It's the archaic, severe, alien-sounding music of technical jargon. He recognizes the characters in this drama—beneficiary, policyholder, insurer—but it's not so easy to identify the relationships the text establishes between them, or, more importantly, its directionality, who gives what to whom, who pays and who charges, what has to happen for so-and-so to do such a thing and such-and-such another. He gets lost in the middle of sentences. Every time he stumbles over an "aforementioned" or a "the same," he has to go back and look for the previous use, but the path is tortuous and he gets lost. The only thing he recognizes is his own name typed in capitals, alone and faltering like an explorer lost in the woods. When he's finished scanning the text, he looks up and meets his mother's eyes, which are wearing an expression of weary impatience. How long has she been looking at him like that, with her turban coming undone on her head at a geologically slow pace, as if it were alive? She wanted his signature, that was all. She didn't think he would read it. But she thought wrong, or she was thinking of someone else. He reads everything. Something need only come to him in writing for his interest to be awoken, no matter whether it's dosage guidelines for medication, a flyer given to him on the street, a furious promise of sodomy scrawled on a bathroom wall, or the series of ominous auspices—fortune and prosperity for those who pass them on; ruin, pain, and failure for those who do not—that begin to appear on notes for five thousand pesos ley, the currency of the day. Why those and not the others is a question he often asks himself. Why not the red ten thousand bill, for example, or the hundred thousand one, with its exotic sheen, on which, though all the notes in the series use the same portrait of General José de San Martín—in three-quarter left-side profile, hair and mustache completely gray and a cravat around his neck: the Liberator in his European exile, confined to a rented room in Boulogne-sur-Mer—he looks slightly older and more bitter than on the fifty-thousand-peso bill and slightly less so than on the two-hundred-thousand-peso one, as if as the denominations rose they accompanied the hero on his journey toward death. Maybe, he thinks, it's because these are the bills in mass circulation, the ones that are used in the commonest transactions; they're the ones that pass through the most hands, and superstitious chains need this kind of fluid circulation in order to spread.

How old must he be the first time he gets one of those marked notes—seven or eight? He's on his way back from a newsstand, where he's just bought himself a little blue block of bitter Suchard chocolate, his favorite candy, and while he's organizing his change he suddenly comes across one of the prophecies written in extravagant biblical syntax that will worry him from that moment on, whether they're frightening or benevolent. *When this note passes into your possession, your luck will change, create seven in its likeness, Judas Thaddaeus ...* How strange it is to read money. And how frightening that your destiny might leap out of it, just as it leaps out of your coffee grounds or the lines on the palms of your hands. He stops next to the stand, slowing the passage of new customers, and while the first piece of chocolate melts in his mouth, he reads the supplication in a very low voice, absorbing, by mere contact with the note, a religious capital that he has never had nor will ever have. *Asunción F., from the Los Roques archipelago, Venezuela, broke this chain and was fired from her job and two months later became sick and lost a leg and died.* The fortunate lives, the stories of salvation—*María Y. wrote this message on seven notes and went to Miami and today she has a house and three beautiful children, one a postmaster and one an engineer*—never have any effect on him. He doesn't even believe them. The tragic ones, on the other hand, have an intolerable realism that makes the whole device plausible. Those notes make such a marked impression on him that on the afternoon eight years later when, partly so as not to upset his mother and her husband, who are devastated by the episode, and partly to check whether what everyone says is true and death is the only thing that can soften the most passionate aversions, he leaves his school uniform on and goes to the dead crostini lover's wake, he can't help asking himself whether that might have been this man's fatal mistake, a man of whom it's not at all clear, today—and the question of what's meant by *today* can be added to all the other unknowns—whether he was a hero or a traitor, fallen in the line of duty or a victim, a soldier or a double agent, a crook out for blood or a family man determined to avoid spilling any: Could it have been breaking a prayer chain that came to him on a lucky note, perhaps not so different from the one that fell into his own hands after he bought his little blue block of Suchard, that caused him to plummet to the bottom of the San Antonio River?

But of course, isn't he himself the perfect counterexample? How many superstitious notes have fallen into his hands since then? Fifty? A hundred? He lets them all pass him by, and he's still healthy, sane, and completely untouched by the massive, grisly tragedies they predict. It's not that he's never considered joining in. He's even got to the point of sitting at the table with a note smoothed out in front of him and a pen in his hand, thinking about how to word his supplication. His own prayer. But he never does it. At the crucial, decisive moment, the idea of entering into such hazardous circulation frightens him more than the consequences of breaking the chain. Still, the idea lingers. He knows he'll never do it, but even so, not a day goes by that he doesn't pay for something and get his change back in small notes—the ones that creep closer to certain extinction with every day, every hour, every second, like endangered species—and start to search them, almost in spite of himself, for some of the illiterate cursive that still manages to be menacing though it's worn by handling; not a day goes by that he doesn't tell himself that someday he'll make up his mind and take the plunge, someday he'll write his prayer and send the note bearing his mark out into circulation, he'll throw it into the anonymous sea of money where it'll shine, unique; and someday, too, no doubt when he least expects it, years, maybe decades later, if the country ever emerges from the black hole that's sucking it in and condemning its cash to periodic deaths, someone will pay him or will give him some change in notes and it'll be like finding a long-lost twin, he'll immediately recognize his own writing, the prayer written on that note by his own hand.

"Don't worry. I don't understand a word of it either," his mother tells him, handing him a pen. "You have to sign down there, above where it says 'Beneficiary.'" He hesitates for a second. He hates his signature. He's hated it ever since the day he first realized he needed one and ended up choosing it hurriedly and without thinking, rushed by the police officer drumming his ink-stained fingers while waiting for him to sign the form to get his ID card. He has always hated it. And while he perfects it—between the first piece of crappy zoo art he decides to put his name on and his membership card for the Communist cinema—his dissatisfaction grows staggeringly complex and refined. Like an artist who invests his talent only in his worst flaws, he's unbelievably faithful to this squiggle that he's so ashamed of, which singles him out wherever he goes: twin lightning bolts, pointing to the right in perfect synchrony, like a pair of ice skaters caught in the middle of a routine. That's him—but he recognizes himself in it even less than in the photos people take of him, which always seem determined, in such a childishly spiteful way, to give him some other idiot's sickly sweet, evasive face.

He signs nevertheless, and the moment he does so he realizes something extraordinary: he's rich. It's true that he realizes it in a slightly abstract way, exactly like the way we understand, with total ease and, moreover, no sense of desperation, that we belong to such an inauspicious category as, for example, that of being mortal. *He's rich* means that he will get two hundred thousand dollars—a hundred thousand for her, another for him, even though he's only his stepfather—if the jumbo jet that takes them to Europe in a week decides to plummet into the middle of the Atlantic, or if a guardrail on the road between Barcelona and Cadaqués permanently interrupts the progress of the 1975 Giulia Sprint that his mother's husband plans to hire to explore the Mediterranean coast. The mere idea of such a catastrophe is appalling, and in the fraction of a second that he spends thinking about it, allowing it to shake him, he sweats five times more than he does while running the fifteen laps of the gym the PE teacher sentences him to for forgetting his sports kit. But death is such a general hypothesis that it grows weak and fades, and moreover is eclipsed by the hypothesis of instantaneous wealth, which is so unexpected and now so near. True: something terrible would have to happen for it to come about. But at the same time, aren't an aerial catastrophe or a lapse of concentration on a mountain road simpler and more accessible routes to wealth, at least for him, who hasn't yet turned fifteen, than a whole lifetime of work, a redemptive business deal, a string of lucky nights at a casino, or a stroke of genius like the one the seven golden men have in the film that teaches him everything he knows and will ever know about bank robbery? Besides, it's precisely the boundless brutality of the

idea that stops him from picturing it, from unfurling a maca-
bre post-collision tableau full of noise, flames, twisted metal,
and severed bodies. (And even so, even though the tableau
is truly unimaginable, some of its ferocity manages to seep
through the cracks between the fingers he's clamped together
over his eyes to avoid seeing it, as he often does at the cinema
during the first shots of surgery or of syringes full of heroin
piercing addicts' veins, and the glimpses of the disaster that
seep through to him always feature his mother in the middle
of the accident, still pinned to her seat by her safety belt, either dying or simply spaced out from the sleeping tablet she
took on takeoff so she could sleep uninterruptedly during the
flight—his mother, who blinks in annoyance, as though wondering who would be so rude as to disturb her sleep like this,
looks around, notices the devastation all around her, and realizes that she's going to die, and after straightening her hair
a little thinks of him, and hopes with all her heart that he will
make good use of the insurance money.) And so he invests all
of the imagination he withholds from the mysterious confla-
gration the policy describes as an accident—the only technical term he remembers, which is just as ancient as the others
but also imbued with a semantic indecision of the type that
could survive any age with its power to disturb intact—in the
idea of being rich—rich, rich, rolling in money!—and in figuring out insurance companies' modus operandi when they put
prices on the lives of the people they insure. If he thinks about
it (and he does, the moment he stamps his monstrous signature on the bottom of the policy, while his mother, abruptly
coming back to life, lets the towel around her head unravel
like a snake and starts to dry her hair with it), why a hundred
thousand dollars and not fifty, three hundred, a million? And
why the same amount for his mother, who never wakes up
before eleven and stays in bed with slices of fresh cucumber
on her eyes and her face smothered in creams until well past

noon, as for her husband, who gets up at dawn and spends his life twisting and turning down muddy country roads surrounded by sick cows, manure, and the smell of disinfectant?

It's as though he's suddenly discovered a new meaning of the phrase *cost of living*. Where else has he seen the species priced in this way? Maybe in films ... slaves in films about Rome, who are bought and sold in town squares for a handful of crude, poorly made coins, or for a few little gilded discs masquerading as coins, which a greedy hand shakes in a bag to make their obscenity ring out like a tambourine. And prostitutes, of course, who are at once so archaic and so auratic, although with them it's never clear whether the price is for the prostitute herself or the package of services she offers. But that's cinema, and he knows all too well how distrustful he must be of anything that impresses him. And besides, with both cases—the slaves under the whip, the women offering their flesh on the street—there's always the same pathos and emotional agitation, a truly cancerous form of extortion that makes it virtually impossible to understand anything. The policy is ruthless in that regard. It doesn't soften emotion, it destroys it. One life equals a hundred thousand dollars. Period. Where else has he seen the orders of the flesh and of money converge like this, with such impassive matter-of-factness? Suddenly, the dead man's voice comes back to him from some distant Sunday lunch, speaking with a terrified tremor. He doesn't see him straight away, something that happens to him often with certain memories: they come back to him lacking a component, such as images, or sounds, or smells, or any of the resonance of the experience, as though someone's intercepted them on their way from the archive to him. But against this momentarily black canvas, he hears his voice repeating a number over and over again in a falsetto, *four million*, the amount that the armed organization that has kidnapped the iron-and-steel company's general manager is demanding by way of ransom, until the picture grows clearer and the dead man appears, utterly beside himself, his whole face bloodshot, gesticulating in his shirtsleeves at a table spread with food that's growing cold, and then taking advantage of the general stupor into which the guests have fallen to stretch out a hand and snatch a crostini. Yes, these numbers tell him something. Much more, in any case, than the phrase *cost of living* in its most common sense, the one everyone uses it in because the price of every single thing and good and service changes from one day to the next, though the crucial question is never answered: why the phrase applies to fluctuations in the price of milk or clothing and not in the price of a captain of the refrigeration industry or an executive at a multinational company.

It's like a fever. Every week the front pages of the papers announce a new record. Four million for the general manager of the iron-and-steel company, a case the dead man knows well, partly because it concerns the corporation he works for, but more because, as he himself says, it hits very close to home, and proves what the discovery of his body at the bottom of the San Antonio River spells out in black and white: how close he is to being next. But there's also the twenty million that the Fuerzas Armadas Revolucionarias demand for Roggio in Córdoba, the five million for the metalworker Barella, the two million three hundred that the Ejército Revolucionario del Pueblo gets out of Lockwood, the million for John Thompson from Firestone, the twelve million Esso pays for Victor Samuelson after five months in captivity. And so on, up to the zenith, the blow to end all blows, the *ne plus ultra* of the flesh–money tariff system, which manages to contain a whole cycle of inflation within itself: the five million that the Montoneros demand when they kidnap the Born brothers in September 1975, and the forty or sixty million—reports vary—that the grain processor Bunge y Born ends up paying out in April 1976, when the executives are finally freed. He follows the dramatic twists in these operations delightedly, as enthusiastically as many of his friends— generally the ones who make fun of him or walk out on him whenever he suggests going to the Communist cinema to see an Eastern European film cycle—follow the local soccer tournament, and is never more jubilant than when the captives regain their freedom and appear, exhausted but happy, on the front pages and in TV news bulletins, surrounded by a cordon of police and cameras. It's not their liberation that moves him, exactly. Neither is it the fact, repeated right and left in the bourgeois press, that with their freedom the prisoners regain the most vital element of life and therefore life itself, which during their captivity in those so-called people's prisons had been reduced to sleeping, pissing, shitting, chewing on some repulsive gruel, walking in circles around tiny rooms, half-hearing their neighbors' radios, and being interrogated. He's not interested in the humiliating miseries of their survival. After all, don't the companies of which these captives are the brains, the figureheads, the proud spokesmen condemn their thousands upon thousands of workers to live precisely the same life, a life that's almost *sub*-life, that all but falls below the minimum threshold of life? And not for the two weeks or three months that they themselves are forced to live it, but for years, whole decades, a whole lifetime, so that for them it's not some perverse substitute for life but life itself, the only one they have, and so the one that, pitiful and foul and inescapable as it may be, demands to be celebrated. No, what delights him, splashed as flagrantly on the newspapers' front pages as the layers of makeup on actors' faces in photos stuck to theater doors, is the transformation that has taken place in the captives. There they are, driving around in the latest cars, flashing tailor-made suits and Italian shoes and signing checks with gold fountain pens, when a perfectly timed commando operation uproots them from their lavish lifestyle. Days, weeks, months later, when they're released and brought before those dazzling flashes, they've turned gray, their scalps have been eaten away by lice, they haven't shaved for weeks, their skin is chafed. They're dirty, they've grown thin, you can see the bones in their faces. They look as defeated as condemned men, and have the glassy-eyed, evasive air of alcoholics, the heavily medicated, victims of abuse. They wear poor-quality sports clothes, outfits improvised from the garments given to them by their captors, all of them mismatched—the shirt untucked, shoes with no laces, nicotine stains on their fingers (those that smoked before being kidnapped carry on puffing like chimneys, and those that didn't adopt the habit with a deadly thirst); their fingernails are broken and dirty, the fingernails of people who've spent every day digging in the vain search for an escape. They're disoriented, they have trouble remembering, they stammer. They look like wild animals or the mentally retarded.

But to him—whose closest encounter with the department of kidnapping and extortion and everything that moves in its orbit (executives at monster corporations, commando units, rifles, people's prisons, hoods, ransoms, fake military uniforms) is the figure *four million*, as yelled by the dead crostini lover in the grip of a wave of terror, and of course the dead crostini lover himself, whom he sees for the last time one summer lunchtime in Mar del Plata, ranting and raving about the garish orange they've painted the chairs at the beach club while filling his mouth with crostini, and then, from one minute to the next, in a dark suit and makeup, squeezed by the narrow walls of a coffin—to *him* the physical and mental deterioration, the loss of energy, and the premature ageing that abductees undergo while they're being held, and which the newspapers feature ecstatically on their front pages, seems to have less to do with the conditions of their captivity, no matter how harsh they are, than with the monetary demand that's imposed on them. The difference between a showy executive soon after his abduction, while he's still in full possession of his faculties, and the same executive when he's released days, weeks, or months later, is monetary. It's the money he's missing, that's been stolen from him; it's the cash flow—because these armed organizations are in his father's camp: they only believe in cash—that's been drained, taking with it all his proteins, nutrients, plasma, red blood cells: all of the basic elements whose evident depletion the police doctors note with alarm when they examine the abductees immediately after their release. He even pictures the whole process in a kind of neat mental cartoon, drawn in that already slightly outdated style—king-size Havana cigars lit with hundred-dollar bills, bulging bellies filled with glassfuls of shrimp cocktail, wristwatches shining like gold ingots—that the radical press often uses to satirize capitalists and their lackeys: the abductee, with his Montecristo still between his fingers, growing thin and fading away in a rickety old bed while a tube that's full to bursting extracts money and blood at once from the same vein.

Once again—as with the life insurance policy his mother makes him sign a week before she sets off for a month and a half in Europe with her second husband—the question is why four million and not two, seven, or a hundred and twenty-five thousand? Once they've seized their target, to use the military jargon that's all the rage at the time, how do the highest-ranking guerrillas work out how much to demand? What criteria do they use, what estimates are they guided by, how do they rationalize this accounting anomaly? If all of these men are rich, why do they ask for seven hundred thousand for some of them and two and a half million for others? Do they ask for the amount they think the enemy can pay, or the amount they need in order to resupply themselves with weapons, communications equipment, vehicles, and hiding places, or to distribute food and clothing in slums and rural wastelands, or to plan future actions? The only thing that's more difficult to price than a human life is art. Whenever he stumbles across one of these exorbitant figures while reading the newspaper, his first feeling is a rush of joy, a euphoric frenzy. When he thinks about poverty, and the misery that has no name, and the terrible hardships that the abductees and the companies they represent force, directly and indirectly, on ever-greater swathes of society, any sum seems too small, any amount ridiculous. There isn't enough money in the world to repay all that! His second impulse is a little different: a slight hesitation, tinged with a certain discomfort. He reads the figure again and thinks: if at least there were some logic to it. If at least it followed the example of Godard-of-no-man's-land, as he christens him on the afternoon he spends buried in a creaky seat at the film archive, stretching his neck as far as he can in an attempt to see over the afros of the couple in front of him; the afternoon he sees the executions in the indoor swimming pool in *Alphaville* for the first time, with the unhappy victims falling into the water in their suits and ties and the party of pinups in bikinis plunging in after them to drag them to the side of the pool; the afternoon he decides, with the solitary solemnity typical of decisions made at fifteen years old, that he will no longer tell the lie everyone tells, calling him the French Godard, the Swiss Godard, even the Swiss-French Godard, because to his mind the border between France and Switzerland is the origin of all that he admires in him, which is to say everything, from his bottle-cap glasses to the cuffs of the narrow-legged pants that are too short for him, not forgetting his women, especially his women, and the bursts of music that erupt like downpours of rain, split the imagery of his films down the middle, and then fall silent again. Godard-of-no-man's-land, who finishes shooting *Tout va bien*, the anticapitalist tract he makes with Jean-Pierre Gorin, and sits down to think, as he does at the end of every film, though now more than ever—precisely because what he's shooting now aren't films but rather anticapitalist tracts, and who the hell is going to pay to get into a cinema to watch one of those, what possible audience could there be for this masterpiece of Kino-Pravda slapstick in which Jane Fonda and Yves Montand play hostages caught in the crossfire of a union dispute—and sets the ceiling at a hundred thousand viewers, the same hundred thousand, he thinks, who go to Père Lachaise for the burial of the militant Maoist Pierre Overney, who was killed at the gates of the Renault factory in Billancourt by the security guard Jean-Antoine Tramoni, without any Lumière brothers present to record the episode. A funeral procession seven kilometers long, a hundred thousand mourners (among them the ugliest philosopher in the world, the one who swears, though he's lying, that he carries everything he needs in his jacket pockets), a hundred thousand cinema seats occupied in Paris.

That's it, that's all he's asking for in the moments when this vertigo strikes him: a system of economy. It doesn't matter what it is. Something that gives some answer to the question of why four million and not two, twenty, or five hundred thousand. It's different with bank robberies, or attacks on police stations or military bases or arms factories. But any ransom request *must* be based on something. Coca-Cola bottles, cars, meter lengths of steel, stocks and shares, undeclared property, offshore bank accounts, livestock, hectares of land … Something! If not, he thinks, if there's no model, no principle of value by which to measure the ransom—no matter how demented it is—there's no solution but to measure it in the worst thing of all: in human life. And if that's the case, how can anyone tell whether the amount requested is a lot or very little?

Who's to say in the case of his mother, for the potential

loss of whose life the insurance company offers a hundred thousand dollars—a hundred thousand greens, as they've already come to be known on the streets, ushering in the financial environmentalism that will pervade public and private conversation over the course of the next two decades— "payable," as he manages to read in the policy before signing it, "on presentation of the corresponding death certificate"? And also, payable how? In their equivalent in pesos? In dollars? And if in dollars, at what exchange rate? The official one, which in April 1975 is set to fifteen pesos and five centavos for every dollar? Or the parallel one, which is more than double that, thirty-six pesos and forty-five centavos? And if it's the parallel rate, from when? From July '75, when in the so-called caves, the offices and agencies where the secret life of money is decided, they're paying sixty-six pesos and five centavos for every dollar? From September, by which time they're paying a hundred and ten? And if it's in pesos, which pesos? The ones from before June 1975, or the ones from afterward, when a bus ticket has gone up by 150 percent and a liter of gas 175? Like everyone else, he finds it difficult to understand the way in which these figures suddenly skyrocket, and in which in produce stores around the city the zeros on the slightly concave violet cartons where the owners chalk up their prices start multiplying dementedly, as though describing some cosmic magnitude—light-years, for example, or expanses of geological time—and not the price of a lettuce, until from one day to the next a law stops them dead and cuts them back down to the ground, and what had cost ten thousand pesos now costs one. But it's even more difficult for him to grasp that the multiplication of those zeros in the price put on the lives of his mother and her husband—when they're on vacation, no less, and at their most relaxed, in the Giulia convertible they hired in Portofino—doesn't necessarily mean that they're worth more, that they're more expensive, that more money will have to be paid out for them if an accident finishes them off.

His mother. At what point does her defiant beauty start to shrivel up? With the devaluation of June '75? Or the even more unexpected one in the middle of July, a coup de grace that wipes out the few survivors left after June? He couldn't say, if he even ever knew. He does remember that on their return from that famous trip to Europe in high season on which—far from being killed by a plane crash, a lapse of concentration, or an attack by one of the many armed organizations ravaging the continent (particularly Italy, where they spend twelve unforgettable sunny days, and Germany, which they're careful to avoid, although less for fear of the Baader-Meinhof group than out of a visceral rejection of all things German, starting with its obscene white-skinned sausages), these apparently being the three main accidents insurance companies take into consideration when drawing up life insurance policies—on their return from that trip on which they spent a good deal of the money that would have come to him if they hadn't been so fortunate, he spots some strange purple parentheses near her temples and under her eyes, as though some tiny arteries had burst beneath her skin and spilled some reddish-black threads. Seeing her, he imagines a crash, a car's brakes being slammed on as if it's collided with something, and the frame of her glasses imprinting itself in her skin. He refrains from asking about them, partly because he hasn't yet recovered from the shock of seeing them both alive again, and on the promised date, after spending hours imagining them suffering all manner of fatal disasters, and partly because he knows full well that if there's one thing his mother cannot tolerate, it's questions or comments about her physical appearance that she herself has not explicitly posed or invited. He's known this for a long time, since the afternoon on the beach in Mar del Plata—with her lying on her side,

greasy from the tanning oil with which she seems to be lac-
quered from head to toe, her head resting on one outstretched
arm and the strap of her bathing suit halfway down the other,
and him fidgeting, desperate to find some moderately comfortable position in which to while away the siesta, a terrible
prison sentence under which he's banned from swimming in
the sea and indeed any physical activity—when he discovers
the shiny, silvery end of a scar poking out diagonally from her
bikini bottoms, and asks her about it, and his mother, without
saying a word, turns onto her stomach and twists her head in
the other direction, like someone in a deep sleep negotiating
the waking world's feeble attempts at sabotage and continu-
ing coolly as they were. That's how it happens: he becomes
aware of his mother's beauty at the very moment that he
perceives a danger to it, just as we become aware of a day's
perfection only when a blackish cloud, dragging itself toward
the sun with reptilian slowness, tinges the electric-blue sky
with fear. And it's not only these purple bunches crowding
around her eyes. Something in her face—probably related to
those marks but vaguer and harder to define—seems to have
expelled his mother from the full, sovereign, arrogant world
that her beauty had permitted her to inhabit: a type of icy
fear, much more icy than her beauty, which has lodged in her
and is making her quake.

In fact, this is also the first time he ever sees her shaking.
She's looking for her keys in her purse, and the moment she
finds them she drops them and then stands motionless for a
fraction of a second, bewildered, with the guilty hand frozen
and shaking very slightly in midair, as though electrified by a
cluster of simultaneous shocks. Every journey toward a glass
of wine becomes unsteady and precipitous; writing a check
ceases to be the child's play it once was. She can no longer answer the phone without making the receiver dance in its cra-
dle, so she begins to turn around and hide her shaking hand

behind her own body, as though protecting it from mocking eyes. One afternoon, under pressure from the super, who's been there for hours fixing the living room blinds and is now hanging about by the door, pretending to examine a loose lock in order to give her time to find a tip, she comes to him to ask for the usual quota of small change, and when she takes it—three small notes, folded in two, with a little stack of coins on top—the trembling cup her hands have formed gives a little, as though it might cave in from the weight.

No, he won't be getting rich from his mother's accidental death, or her husband's. Not in that ignoble way—which much later, when he remembers those two months in 1975 and relives the excitement that flooded him every time the phone rang and he discovered that his mother and her husband were setting out on another flight, or getting back into the Giulia to go from one little town on the Côte d'Azur to the next, fills him with incomparable shame—nor any other, since he will always be useless not so much at earning money—because he will earn it, and sometimes in considerable sums, although always completely hopelessly, only realizing how considerable they are once he's made them vanish, disappear into thin air, squandered them, not a fucking cent in the coffers, zero—as multiplying it or just keeping it as it is, intact, safe from any eventuality, beyond history, like an egg in a gene bank, a trophy in a club's display cabinet, or a work of art in a museum. He would give everything he doesn't and won't ever have to know how to *make* money. Literally make it, produce it, like employees of the mint, or former employees who—later or even while still working there—become counterfeiters; or *make it appear*, like his father does, in fact, two Fridays of every month for years, between eleven at night and seven thirty the next morning, when he *has a table booked*—the turn of phrase he himself uses for his poker nights once they've been made common knowledge within the family—and also on his visits to the casino in Mar del Plata, lightning-fast excursions that also always begin on a Friday (one of the two left after those when he has a table booked), real raids of frenzied, compulsive gambling that start when he sets out, always in a taxi, on the 404 kilometers from the office at Maipú and Córdoba, right in the center of Buenos Aires, to 2100 Boulevard Marítimo Patricio Peralta Ramos, where he spends on average seven hours gambling ceaselessly—never playing roulette, which is for amateurs; it's always baccarat or blackjack, sometimes baccarat and blackjack at the same time; seven hours without eating or sleeping and sometimes without even standing up to stretch his legs, fueled by whiskey and cigarettes, while the taxi driver—the same boy from Tucumán his ex-father-in-law hired to follow him, who lent him the six hundred pesos that helped him turn around that famous bad table—waits for him a few blocks away with the radio on, head nodding sleepily in a car parked by the square.

As for him, if there's one thing he knows how to do with money, it's pay. That's the only thing he can boast about, pathetic as it is. He accepts this as the role assigned to him in an arbitrary but indisputable allocation. His lot is not to make money, like his father does, or to inherit it, like his mother. Of all the possible missions, his is to settle the books, be the one who clears accounts. Some people feed the hungry, others cure the sick. His way of healing wounds—a passion that's not always very well understood—is paying. He assumes the role with the same resigned conviction with which he states his star sign—the one that gets by far the worst press in the whole zodiac—whenever he's asked (generally by women, women he doesn't want and who want him more than any he might ever want); but even so he performs it with an inexplicable satisfaction, in a state of euphoria, feeling like he does when, after exhausting his oxygen reserves with a lengthy exploration of the tiled bottom of a swimming pool, he pushes his head out of the water and uses the last of his energy to open his mouth wide and fill himself with lungfuls of air. There's always a strange urgency in paying, no matter whether he's on time or not: a suspense that seems to contradict the rather submissive nature of the act. While his friends steal money from the coats their parents leave hanging on the rack or siphon it from their monthly allowance to buy records, beer, clothes, cigarettes, and maybe a few hour-long sessions at seedy hotels, he, when he gets his first bit of money, the money he earns from his first job—which is to translate an article on the epicurean eccentricities of an English playwright who twenty years later, after he's been ravaged by stomach cancer, wins the Nobel Prize—uses it in part, but as a matter of priority, to pay a months-old debt to a classmate, a rich, forgetful young satrap who once got him out of one of his not-infrequent tight spots—his mother having yet again secretly taken the money he had put aside for the next day's food after finding herself short of cash in the small hours of the night—by paying for his lunch; a classmate who is of course most surprised when he tries to return the money, the loan and also the lunch having disappeared from his memory without trace. He hesitates. In two seconds, everything he could do with the money if he didn't return it passes before his eyes, all the things it singles out and burnishes with its light and renders possible and that now suddenly start trying to tempt him, like dazzling sirens, at the door of the terrible steakhouse where he's trying to return the money that was lent to him, the same place where months earlier he invested it in a withered salad and a rump steak that he left half eaten. But he's so close to paying, so close to closing something that's been open for such a long time . . . How could he fail to follow through when he's this close, when he's come this far? That would be squandering par excellence, one luxury he can't allow himself. Of course, what kind of repayment is it when even his creditor can't remember the debt he swears he's incurred? He doesn't remember the episode, or how much he lent him, none of it. Not the rump steak, or the salad, or the clothes he assures him he was wearing that day—gym pants with knees made stiff by generation upon generation of mending, a white piqué T-shirt, the regulation blazer with the sleeves tied around his neck, like a parody of a scarf. It's useless: there's no way to make him remember. And then, partly so that he can feel that he's doing everything in his power, like Kafka's man before the law, and partly dragged along by the insistence of his own memory, he lets himself get carried away by the details of that lunchtime of whose occurrence even he is not now entirely sure, perhaps it's just a pretext created by his desire to satiate himself by paying. Spring: the windows at half-mast, the smell of *carne asada* in the air, the television tuned in to a gossip show, the blades of the ceiling fans turning endlessly. In walks the girl from the third year who all the boys in the fifth are in love with—the boss-eyed one who's killed beside the train tracks three weeks after the coup d'état—displacing a cloud of air that hits him in the face like a slap, and asks for a *tortilla de papas* to take away (she's as prickly as a beggar and always eats her lunch alone underneath the staircase at school); then she turns back to face the dining room and, resting her elbows on the counter like a girl from a Western looking for trouble, looks them both in the eyes, both of them at once. The other guy thinks for a few seconds and shakes his head, but he takes the money all the same. They go into the steakhouse, which is still deserted, and sit down. "Get what you like," he says. "It's on me."

Yes, paying, and all of its attendant sibylline delights: turning around and walking away from the cashier's window with his heart still in his mouth, as though he's just received a pardon, and putting the precious stamped receipt safely in his pocket with an excitement he's barely able to conceal, and later on stapling it—that adorable crunch!—to the bill, crossing it off his list of debts, and, finally, filing it away in the clear plastic file where, one by one, his receipts from accounts paid all end up, each one a trophy of a vice that he never dares to share with anybody. This all strikes him as so contemptible and miserly that he'd find it very difficult to confess; it's like the pleasure a bank teller takes in tracing and savoring the dirty scent of money on his fingertips, or a night guard in spotting couples on the garage's security cameras. And afterward, once the receipt's been filed away, comes the feeling that he can start again from zero: he's young again, virginal, free to look for the next payment on the list ... Though it's hard to believe, this bureaucrat's pleasure is the thing that excites him most about living on his own for the first time—much more than the possibility of organizing his time and space as he wishes, without having to answer to anybody, or the freedom to invite over whomever he wants, whenever he wants, for whatever reason he wants. Just that: paying his bills, much more than all the things that are normally understood by sovereignty, at a time—he's just turned twenty-one—when after four crushing years of terror, the experience of sovereignty survives only in the private realms of life, in homes, bedrooms, basements, rooms as far as possible from the street and public life. For him, gaining his freedom, a phrase that's been emptied of all meaning apart from the individual departure from the nest, primarily means discovering an unexpected form of alchemy that makes a typical adolescent nightmare pleasurable, even glorious: Will I have enough money to pay the bills every month? Paying, paying: the principal enjoyment of the adult life he's trying on for the first time. What a joy to arrive at the beginning of the month and have to pay.

There's nobody else in the world who can keep time's accounts like his father does. His father, who will die without a penny, broke, as they say, leaving half a dry lemon and a withered lettuce in the fridge and a collection of dusty jazz records on two shelves held up by bricks, and taking his mental calculator to the grave with him, having never, even for a second, stopped shuffling quantities with it, or adding and multiplying years and money; calculating ages, the duration of marriages, flight times, and time differences between countries; converting dollars to pesos, pesos to dollars, official dollars to black-market dollars; figuring out the attendance at protests, soccer matches, film screenings; predicting the commercial success of new theatrical undertakings; or prorating ticket-office takings according to numbers of cinema screens. *He*, of course, is always quick to lose count, but what he does know is that years later—at least ten or fifteen—it's not just on the first of each month that he gets to enjoy the pleasure of paying, but rather, to his delight, every Friday of every week, four times a month—"like clockwork," per his father's description of the regularity with which he does three things in life: shit, fuck, and play poker—for the eleven never-ending months it ends up taking to refurbish the apartment he buys fifty-fifty with his wife—two and a half times longer than the time frame the architect quoted without hesitation at the beginning of the project. Every Friday at half past six or seven in the evening, he runs up those three long flights of stairs with his pockets bursting with cash. The contractors are in the apartment's living room, smoking while they wait for him surrounded by wooden beams and piles of bricks. He comes in, greets them with a monosyllable and a nod of the head—the same currency they use to communicate with him for the duration of the job, whether they like him or not—and sits down in the kitchen, or rather the dilapidated hovel where according to the architect's drawings there will someday be something resembling a kitchen, and with a wad of notes in his hand, he shouts, "First one's up!"

Thus begins the weekly round of payments. And so it is, every Friday.

Anyone else in his position would have exploded already. Not just because of the way the completion date keeps being pushed back, which is annoying and even slightly insulting in light of the smile and the slaps on the back the architect tries to placate him with every time he asks for explanations, distracting him by pointing out sheets of colored mosaic tiling, the antique floor tiles he found at the salvage yard, and the period toilets waiting their turn in a corner, three apparently more than sufficient justifications for him to accept the delays, even to enthusiastically approve them, as the price he must pay for the inspiration and good taste of a sublime architect. In fact, the truly hellish thing is the inflationary disaster in which the country is burning up day by day, which surges a fortnight after work begins, accompanies the refurbishment from beginning to end, sending the agreed budgets into orbit and making a mockery of every estimate, and will outlive the project by a year and a half, an insane period during which it devours everything that gets in its way, not only his money, his time, his nerves, and his already fragile relationship with the architect, but also his love. Love: the only reason he put all his money—the only money he has or will ever have, aside from that which literally comes out of the past, like a ghost, raining down on him on the very same afternoon that he has to cremate his father—into the purchase of an apartment that is what's known as an opportunity: underpriced, immediate sale, almost abusive terms of payment, which the seller accepts without saying a word. But these benefits are no compensation for the problems he and his wife discover later, when, exhausted by eleven nightmarish months of construction, they move in and experience for themselves the fierce hostility of the neighbors (all more than seventy-five years old, all deaf), the vibration of the machinery in the textile business next door against the apartment's south wall from eight in the morning until five in the afternoon, the neighborhood's unreliable drains, the criminals-in-training who meet on the corner, the piles of broken glass from car windows gleaming by the side of the curb, the always-out-of-date goods at the local stores, the smell of rotting in the produce stores and insecticide in the bars, the sparse bookshops, the outdated film screenings, the faded posters in the video shop, and above all the unbearable, almost radioactive heat that melts the treeless roads and beats down all summer long on the building's leaky roof terrace—which is to say, on the roof of the brand-new home that they don't even manage to share for two months.

Prices change overnight, from hour to hour, sometimes two or three times in the same hour. Sometimes he comes back from the building supply store empty-handed, having been unable to buy anything. "We don't have any prices," they tell him. Other times—and this happens very often—he counts out the cash he owes while he's lining up in front of the register, but when he gets to the window he has to calculate it all again. The price has gone up 10, 15, sometimes 20 percent in the tiny interval—no more than ten, fifteen minutes—between the last markup and his turn to pay. The same thing happens every Friday afternoon, ten, sometimes five minutes before the financial institutions close, when he turns up with his weekly installment of dollars in the usual filthy den in the business district, the lair of a money changer his father trusts, an affable man who's suffocating under his own weight, and who takes advantage of each of his visits to draw him away from the line and, lowering his voice to the confidential tone people usually use to reveal the secret of the country's economic future, bombard him with stories of his father's other life, his real, completely fantastical life, which when he relays them to him just as he heard them, his father is evidently a little disconcerted to hear, neither accepting nor denying anything but, finally, smiling and saying he doesn't remember anything about it. And just like that, in the few minutes it takes this legendary father to clean out a sheik in Monaco, or break the bank in Baden-Baden, or get locked up for claiming responsibility for the urine with which a tourist in his charge decides to leave his mark on the ruins of Pompeii, the peso has depreciated so vertiginously that the pockets of the jacket he wore especially for the occasion, which were tried and tested in the same basement the previous Friday, in front of the same redheaded cashier who counts money with one hand while peeling the other's cuticles with his teeth, can't accommodate the heap of australs he receives in exchange for his dollars.

It's impossible to keep up. Nobody is fast enough. When construction work begins, the largest banknote in circulation is a thousand pesos, and to try to get change from one is a true odyssey. By the time it's finished eleven months later, there are already five- and ten-thousand-peso bills going around, reigning like monarchs, young, distant, and untouchable, and then four weeks later, when they're as common as the commoners over which they once reigned, they disappear without fanfare in the purchase of a few basic items. You can't even name amounts without getting something wrong. There's *palo*, meaning a million, which he hears for the first time more than ten years earlier in one of the surreptitious conversations at the crostini lover's wake aimed at figuring out how much the dead man was carrying in the famous attaché case—*a palo of dollars, at least*, is the precise phrase that reaches him through the jangling of spoons against coffee cups; and now there's a new one: *luca*, meaning a thousand pesos, coined partly as an abbreviation, and probably partly in the hope that the shift from the domain of numbers to that of words will calm the expanding chaos that is the universe of money, will somehow confine and control it, at least inasmuch as everyday language can ever control what is mute, has nothing to say, and can only grow up and down at the same time, like Alice when she falls down the hole. But how soon *luca* loses its original luster and begins to sound cheap. How quickly it's replaced, not by other notes, but by other names, cheap, spontaneous inventions that are always slightly childish and immediate, like *a red, a green, a blue*, names inspired by the colors of the notes, which taxi drivers, salesmen, and cashiers begin to use routinely alongside old and disappearing denominations, as in, *that's two lucas, a red, and two blues*, for example, or *gimme a luca and I'll give you three greens*—shows of primitive pedagogy that do nothing but confuse everybody.

It's crazy. Some days he has to go to five separate building supply stores—each a long way from the last and usually in remote parts of the city, so that he wastes hours traveling between them—before ending up not at the best one, nor at the one that's been recommended to him, nor even at the cheapest one, but simply at one that can give him a price—a price that he is able to pay, which, by this stage, with the cost of living rising by 150 percent every month, means a price that's unacceptable within reason—and where they haven't followed the example of most building supply stores and decided to hoard all their goods and wait for prices to go up again: bricks, sand, cement, whatever the mobs of project managers, architects, and construction workers who knew about the place before him haven't already taken. He finds the place, goes in, and finally gives his order, flooded with happiness but also trembling, so acute is his awareness that the immediate future of the work depends on the response he gets from the foreman, which will be one of three things: yes, they have everything he needs, and the price doesn't irredeemably compromise his already decimated quote, and everyone's happy; or yes, they have everything, et cetera, but when it's time to pay they don't ask for pesos—which is what he carries on him, out of prudence more than practicality, since, sign of the times, the mere suspicion that someone is carrying a handful of foreign notes is enough to make them a target—but dollars, dollar bills, the currency in which 80 percent of store owners have by this point taken refuge, and in which they'll remain entrenched even when there's no longer any reason to be, a bit like the televisions that show up in bars along with the first World Cup games and end up becoming part of the furniture. If they require dollars, *cash verde*, and he doesn't want to lose his order and put a stop to the construction work, he'll have to find them before the store closes, which means by six o'clock at the latest, and given that banks and currency exchanges have been closed for half an hour already, this means he'll have to track them down in sordid local malls, back rooms of sham travel agencies, bar restrooms, parking lot stairways, all the secret dens where the *arbolitos*, or little trees, as they call themselves, to match the dollar's vegetal green—members of an underclass who come out only after the banks and currency exchanges have pulled down their shutters, looking to earn their living by buying and selling when there's no rate of any type to be had, either the official one or the accepted black-market one; when there's a totally free market on the dollar—have been blooming for months, stationed behind columns to smoke, or walking in circles, seeming idle at first glance but in fact with all of their senses alert, prickling for the arrival of desperate people like him. In time he learns to recognize them straight away, too, even right there at the building supply store, where they've infiltrated the line and the notes they plan to sell at astronomic prices are growing warm in their pockets.

How does he not break down? Most nights, he can't sleep, and in the still half-light of dawn he feels the day nibbling at him before it's even begun. He foresees everything that might go wrong, the things he'll fail to get, the opportunities that will pass him by unnoticed or that he'll be unable to take. He can see it all so clearly and in so much detail that ten minutes later his head starts to fizz. He's sitting up in bed, rigid and covered in sweat, his mouth dry, already wondering not how he'll get back to sleep, but how he'll manage to poke a toe out of the sheets and put it on the ground and begin, get going. If only he were bulletproof, like his father. If only he had his agility, his flexibility, the mixture of indifference and sangfroid with which he makes his way through this minefield. If it weren't for his father, in fact, there would be no apartment, no renovation, no architect, no gang of taciturn construction workers to summon every Friday to the forbidding pit that someday, if the architect is to be believed, will be a kitchen, where he performs the ritual of paying, the only thing he knows how to do, and the only thing that saves him from going crazy over the course of those eleven hellish months.

Because it's to his father that he decides to entrust his money, without giving it a second thought—his father, who, to judge by the familiarity with which he moves through this world, sees little difference between the maneuvers used in financial speculation and those he's learned from years of casino visits. Though in fact it's not exactly his money—since he doesn't have a single peso that's truly his own—but a gift he receives out of the blue one day from his mother's husband, who apparently attaches little importance to it, seeming to have no other motive than the idea of a "living inheritance" following the sale—or *cashing out*, in the translation his father gives on receiving the parcel of money, literally a parcel, since what he gets is the wad of notes exactly as the currency exchange office gave it to his mother's husband and his mother's husband to him: wrapped in brown paper, tied around its length and breadth with the same plastic string bakeries use to tie up packets of pastries—of the collection of things, fields, livestock, and farming machinery he gets after his mother's death.

Ten thousand dollars. It's the first cash he's had in his life—real, noteworthy cash; cash and not wages, remuneration, or payment for services rendered—and it doesn't come from the people from whom natural order or the law might dictate that he'd receive it—his father, his mother—but rather from someone who has no legal obligation to him, who would have been entirely within his rights to spend the whole fortune on himself—*blow it*, in his father's words—and not invite him to the party. Although he does blow it nonetheless, with the unwavering help of his wife and number-one business partner, his mother—who in turn contributes her share of the proceeds from the sale of the steel factory her father leaves behind when he dies—over the course of the following ten or fifteen years: trips, bad investments, bold but ill-conceived business ventures, hesitations the country does not forgive, and, above all, the lengthy construction of the Beast (as it comes to be known less than three months after work begins, with a clairvoyance that probably merited more attention), their house-building project on the Uruguayan coast, a true *coup de foudre* that keeps them locked in blind, unconditional complicity, like the bond between two souls planning and executing a long-cherished crime, and which then grows out of all proportion, and out of their grasp, and finally turns against them, bleeds them dry, and destroys them.

Though it's hard to believe, ten thousand dollars go to him. That translates to a hundred and forty thousand pesos in January, when his mother's husband gives them to him, and nineteen million five hundred thousand in December, when the apartment in which he'll sleep for less than two months has sucked all but the last centavo out of him. He never really recovers from the shock. The line about the living inheritance doesn't convince him. He thinks there must be something else. If it's some bizarre code of ethics on being a stepfather, he'd like to know about it, and maybe what its principles are. He's wary. What if the money is just the visible part of a plan he knows nothing about, and by accepting it he's committing to a life he doesn't want? But his mother's husband doesn't give any explanations—he's not a big talker—and, despite his worst fears, he's more respectful of him and takes more of an interest in his affairs than ever after giving him the money. Meanwhile, his mother, whether out of objection, or jealousy, or because her husband's decision surprised her as much as it did him, takes every opportunity to let him know that she was responsible—not directly, because they never spoke about it, but by a sort of osmosis, using her private, every-day influence, which then explains a multitude of otherwise inexplicable things—for making sure that that *pile of cash*, as she calls it—and from the way the phrase twists her mouth it's obvious that this is the first time she's used it—went to him and not a fixed-term dollar account, another property in Uruguay, a brand-new Japanese car, or the most expensive tournament pass to the tennis club in Forest Hills, including a five-star hotel and first-class flights. She tells him this when he first receives the money, naturally, but she also carries on telling him after that, eternally, so that he can never forget: when he uses it to renovate the apartment he plans to share with his wife, and later on, after the separation, when he and his ex-wife sell the newly renovated apartment and he broken-heartedly spends all the money, *blows* it—him, too!—on a trip to Europe that couldn't be more depressing, and even much much later, when the little matter of the living inheritance has been totally forgotten, is off the agenda, and his mother and her husband separate after thirty-five years of marriage in the midst of calamitous financial and emotional bankruptcy, made mortal enemies by, among many other things, the way in which the construction of the Beast has eaten away at them over the almost fifteen years they've spent dealing with it. But he knows it's not true. He knows that there's only one person who's responsible for this decision, extravagant as it is, and it's his mother's husband; that it's to him and his secret reason for making this decision, be it love, generosity, an attempt at bribery, or idiocy, pure and simple, that he is and always will be indebted.

One thing that's for certain is that as soon as he has the money in his power, he rejects outright the investment options his mother's husband insists on offering him—livestock, premium semen pills, plots of fertile land outside the city: the very burdens he's just happily rid himself of in favor of cold, hard cash and the freedom, in his own words, to dispose of it whenever he likes—and gives it to his father to take care of. He trusts his father. He even trusts him in the face of the scandalized skepticism he meets from his mother, who when she finds out gives her most sarcastic laugh and tells him very well, wonderful, but it would have been safer to put it on the horses at the Palermo tracks or invest it in stamps or subway tokens, and then informs him that if some disaster should occur—at which point a lush catalog of catastrophes seems to pass before his shining eyes—he won't get any more from them.

What his father does with the money is a mystery. He doesn't tell him, and he prefers not to ask, convinced that if he finds out, his life will be made impossible by worrying about its fate. He also develops a superstition: he thinks that if he ignores the game his money's participating in, he can neutralize the irrational nature of that game, or magically tip it in his favor. The only thing he knows, because it's the first thing his father tells him, is that for the five months his money's put to work—during which time, he says, his capital will achieve the highest return the black market can offer—there will be no receipts or documentation, nothing official, signed, sealed, or dated; none of the stuff that would come with a fixed-term deposit at a bank or other financial institution to prove that the money exists and is earning dividends somewhere and belongs to him. He also knows that, strictly speaking, the fact that he gives his father a wad of a hundred new hundred-dollar bills doesn't mean anything at all, and neither is there any meaning in the fact that his father puts it in his inside jacket pocket just as it is, without unwrapping it or counting it, as though he had been expecting it for years. It's not his father's hands that he's placing the money in, a truth his father confirms before his very eyes some twenty minutes later in a European airline's office, when he approaches the employee at the register, a young woman in a flight attendant's uniform with the remains of old eyeliner on her eyelids, and after the obligatory swaggering, double entendres, and jokes that make her blush—the flirting routine that he's been watching in action since he was a child accompanying his father on his work errands in the business district every Friday, and which he now sees as his father's second language, a basic but crucial tongue without which none of his necessary daily transactions would turn out as happily as they seem to—his father plucks the ten thousand dollars he's just given him from his inside jacket pocket and settles an account.

Trusting him means trusting that he knows whom to trust. His father is a link in a chain, a recruiter of cash. Without him, that money—though it's only a modest sum—would never enter the game. But the chain is long and winding, and he doesn't know the other links, and they probably don't and won't ever know one another, not because it's safer that way or out of a desire to preserve hierarchies—these being the most common explanations for the obsession with compartmentalization that underlies the logic of many secret organizations, among them the armed organization that is said to have crashed the helicopter carrying the dead crostini lover, along

with the attaché case full of money and the pilot—but because they're linked by nothing more than a number, a purely
nominal entity, in this case ten thousand dollars, or to put it
another way, one more among the millions of anonymous
figures that set the game in motion and keep it going. This
is all he needs to know about the logic of finance, a magma
that will always fascinate and elude him. No, there's no such
thing as "his" money; "his mother's husband's money"
doesn't exist, nor "his father's." Money isn't personal, it isn't
property, it doesn't belong to anybody. Money is what's always there before money. It's a boundless ocean, nothing but
horizon, into which millions of wads just like his flow every
second, from every direction, losing their identities the moment they plunge in and surviving for months in a state of total formlessness and amnesia, every trace of their origin and
even any quantity distinctions having been wiped out; in the
best-case scenarios they return to being what they once were
when a shore appears out of nowhere and, from it, someone
remembers them and recognizes them and returns them to
everyday circulation, enriched by the scars left by danger and
adventure.

That's the best-case scenario. In the worst, which is also
the most frequent when the country is caught in the cen-
trifugal force of a so-called *inflationary spiral*, the money is
lost and disappears forever, is swallowed by the common
ocean and only reminds the world of its existence when its
owner—who awaits it anxiously for the agreed period and
then, once that's over, carries on waiting in vain for weeks or
months more, knocking on doors that never open, dialing
disconnected phone numbers, hunting down employees who
are stunned by this madman they've never seen before—
realizes that he's lost it all, leaves his jacket folded neatly on
a bench at the station, and hurls himself onto the subway
tracks. More than once during those five months, after being

startled by the parade of bloodbaths he reads about in the newspapers—bankruptcies, banks folding, fugitive directors of finance companies, small investors who've been conned rioting until the police come and disperse them—he begins to feel a little like that furious man holding his hand to his forehead like a visor and desperately searching the open sea for some trace of his money. If he isn't that man, if he just feels like him, that's only because his father knows how to calm him down. His father brings the subject up before he does, as a topic of conversation rather than a source of terror, talking about the cash with a mixture of nostalgia and admiration, as though remembering a much-loved and very sensible relative who at a certain age decided on a change of life and is now the center of all manner of thrilling intrigues in far-off countries, which will change them forever but from which they'll return safe and sound and even improved, stronger, capable now of facing the monsters they once fled. And having brought it up unbidden, he abandons it again just as easily, filing it away and returning to the routine they've shared for twenty years: a while at the office, then lunch at the fake Italian restaurant at Esmerelda and Córdoba, coffee in a bar at Florida and Paraguay, his rounds of airlines, agencies, and currency exchanges, a visit to the bookshop in the basement of the Jardín mall, goodbyes in Plaza San Martín.

Seeing him going about his business so naturally, his fears dissolve. He figures none of this could be happening if his money were in danger. At least one habit would have to change. His father wouldn't eat as quickly as he always does, pitting himself against an invisible opponent. He wouldn't clean his plate with little pieces of bread and then throw them in his mouth. He wouldn't joke about soccer with the maître d'. He wouldn't leave his customary exorbitant tips. He wouldn't stop to look at shoes in a shop window. He wouldn't discuss the Finance Ministry's announcements in the distant, sarcastic tone of someone who knows they don't apply to him, as though he came from a foreign country. Somehow this energetic, slightly restless normality soothes him. No matter what happens, things always find a way to run their own course. And so he ends up forgetting about the money, and when he's reminded of it by something he wants or suddenly realizes he needs, something that costs more than he carries in his pocket or keeps in the old shoebox in his wardrobe, the blow has a visible effect on him, and he feels a stab of frustration, but his discomfort eases as soon as he sees this missing money for what it is: a homeland he's had to leave for reasons of force majeure, though he remains committed to it and it awaits him with open arms, more opulent than ever.

This lasts for five months. Until one day while getting out of a taxi his mother realizes that, as usual, she doesn't have any small change—a phrase she uses only when she's the one who doesn't have it—and asks him to pay, and then has a sudden moment of illumination right there on the sidewalk and asks him if he shouldn't be getting his money back right around now. At the time, he lets himself be drawn in by the mockery poisoning his mother's tone, and then ignores it in order to take his mind off his fear, just like he does every time something shocks him. But later, when they've said their goodbyes and his mother turns and begins to walk away slowly, with her already slightly tired gait, her arms hanging almost still by her sides, and her head held low, as soon as he's safely out of her sight, the first thing he does is open his diary and flick as fast as his anxious fingers will go through days already lived, bills paid, and bar napkins full of to-do lists that he emptily promises himself he'll transfer to the diary, until finally he's looking at the page for that day and at the crucial hour ringed with a fluorescent circle and surrounded by large exclamation marks, like an inspired chess combination—and he discovers that his mother is right. Today's the day. How, why she's so mindful of the date he's supposed to get his money back, even though he thought he'd taken great care to keep this information from her, having foreseen the toxic use she could make of it, he doesn't know. His mother always seems to be bragging that she knows everything about his father and him, the double act that comes together as rapidly as the marriage breaks down (which is to say very rapidly), and in particular that she knows all about the things they hide from her, that she knows about them before they've even happened, and though she often gets it wrong and ends up putting two and two together and getting five, and taking as given things that exist only in her own imagination, he's not insensible to the conviction with which she lets him know that she knows; it always makes him founder and doubt himself, makes him double- and triple-check things he was sure of, things he'd confirmed seconds before meeting her. This is probably the only thing she has left of the unfortunate, fleeting kingdom the three of them once shared, and she carries it everywhere with her: a certain bent for suspicion; the desire to know what the enemy is plotting.

Ten days later, he has the money again—in cash. He doesn't get it back at once, all together, as he had expected, but rather bit by bit, in four installments, first two small ones, wrapped in newspaper, and then two larger ones in brown paper bags, some of it in heaps of Argentine money, some of it in dollars, the smallest and most wrinkled notes mixed with larger, newer ones, among them some so new and so crisp that he wonders whether he's being given freshly counterfeited money. They're rapid transactions, with no preamble nor any particular show of emotion, which his father carries out as if he doesn't want to leave any trace of them, briskly and in all the normal settings: the office; a bar full of cooking smells and staff with dandruff gesticulating in their shirtsleeves; even the street door to his building, where his father briefly stops the taxi he's passing in, hands him the final packet of cash through the window, without getting out, and goes on his way, giving him no time to react, not even to say thank you. Broken up like this, the handover leaves a vaguely disappointing taste in his mouth. Which isn't so bad, after all that's happened. As is often the case with trivial but unexpected feelings, which can eclipse much stronger but more predictable ones simply because they come as a surprise, the disappointment dulls and dispels his anxiety, which is what he should reasonably have felt when his father originally told him that the return of his money would be staggered. But the urgent, scatterbrained, sloppy nature of the collection also blunts his relief at having recovered the money and, more importantly, the happiness he should feel at the miracle of its multiplication. He has almost three times what he started with, much more than anyone else could or does make by putting the same initial amount in a bank at the same time, while he gets his fingers dirty counting his small fortune. It's a pity that the miracle withers a little when he spreads the cash out on the table and contemplates an assortment of piles, sizes, colors, currencies, and textures that don't go together and will never—and this is what makes him saddest—have the unity, the wholeness of the original bundle of dollars, scrawny as it was.

He'd like to thank him, at least. He seeks him out in the next few days, asks him to lunch, to see a film, to meet him for a drink. He could swear that his father is avoiding him. The few times he does see him, always at the office, the only place he can be sure of ambushing him, and always hurriedly, because every single time, his father has to get to a meeting or has people waiting for him, he takes advantage of the few minutes he has and talks. At the mere mention of the money, his father busies himself with something else—a phone ringing in a nearby office; the mess of bar napkins covered in scrawling, coffee receipts with notes on the back, and phone numbers written on bits of ripped newspaper that he calls *my diary*—or frowns and even seems to get annoyed, like those very modest or very vain people who love recognition when it takes them by surprise, but who get prickly about praise for talents they already know they have.

He'll have to wait years to find out the truth behind his father's behavior: until his father is in the last stage of life—last in the strictest sense, meaning the stage of hospitalization, because as soon as he's admitted to the hospital and he sees the retinue of doctors and nurses crowding around him—him, the man who's set foot in a medical practice only twice in seventy-two years, and both times for the most extraneous reasons, to collect payment for some tickets to Cancún the first time and a poker debt the second—he knows there's no going back, that he'll only be exiting this stage feetfirst. Though it's true that the explanation comes from his father, out of his mouth, one night when it's his turn to sit beside the bed, it's not exactly his father who confesses. It's not the same man who comes to the hospital of his own accord a week earlier, in any case. That man is very tired and bathed in sweat. His thighs are cramping up with a pain like nothing he's ever felt before, and his blood pressure's through the roof, but he's also sufficiently with it to stop the taxi without interrupting the sermon on soccer and politics with which he's been persecuting the driver, a combination he excels in and to which his blood pressure is particularly sensitive. His reaction to the dizziness that overcomes him in the street—the latest in a series of episodes he's been keeping secret—proves that he's still in his right mind: he goes straight to the hospital—an absolutely astonishing decision for him, given the disdain he's always so famously professed for the medical world, and the equally famous good health, or pride, that has enabled him to manage without his son—and after arriving and being confined to a wheelchair that he initially rejects but is soon thrilled by, like a bad-tempered child who's figured out how to turn some stupid adult treasure against its owners, he objects to every method by which the doctors propose to stabilize him, treating them as though they're completely useless, fleeing them in his chair, and launching himself at full speed down the ramps in the emergency room. Between the wild, irascible man who checks in to that citadel of medicine of his own will and drives its residents crazy, and the glassy-eyed ghost who suddenly starts remembering everything aloud in the intensive care unit where he spends almost two weeks (how he was never sure whether he'd be able to get the money back; how many times during those ten days he nearly called him to confess that he had lost it all; how many he felt he couldn't face it and considered disappearing off the face of the earth), there come an angioplasty to which he submits with contagious and belligerent good cheer, the disastrous coronary symptoms that flare up as a result of the angioplasty, and almost five hours of open-heart surgery, five hours of brutal butchery from which it's not clear to anybody how he will recover, if he's lucky enough to, and from which he does ultimately recover a minimal kind of life, stuffed full of tubes and with his chest slit from throat to diaphragm and wrapped in a corset made of bandages that are soon soaked with blood.

He's the one keeping his father company on the night three or four days after the operation when a nurse announces with a smile that stretches from ear to ear that they've taken the ventilator away to see if he can manage on his own. He came to the hospital just to come, because there's nothing else he can do, not because he thought it would be useful. He's only allowed in the room intermittently, for half an hour out of every two. He spends the rest of the time in the waiting area, dozing and reading in its bad light, and is flooded with surprise and envy when he sees the camping kit—thermos,

blankets, a little plastic cooler, board games, a nightstand—
his neighbors unpack for their vigil, proving themselves to be
either less shortsighted or more experienced than him in the
matter of hospitalization. All he wants is to be in the room. As
soon as a nurse reminds him of visiting hours and he leaves
it for the dull light of the waiting area, he begins to yearn for
the starry, throbbing darkness in which his father lies sleeping, as though it were some strange kind of paradise, a chilly,
modern kingdom full of mechanical emotion and electronic
diversions. Then an hour and a half later, when they let him in
again, he feels nothing but desolation: sadness; helplessness;
an awful, bloodsucking boredom. There's nothing he can do.
He'd like to touch his father, but he doesn't know where; it's
impossible to reach his body through all the tubes, catheters,
and wires. And he might not touch him even if he did know.
He's terrified that any gesture, let alone a loving one, could
irreversibly alter the extremely delicate equilibrium that's
keeping him alive. There aren't even any chairs in intensive
care—they've thought of everything that might keep visitors
away—so he dozes standing up, clutching the book he won't
read because there isn't enough light.

At one point he thinks he hears a noise coming from his
father, the tail end of a human phrase, and opens his eyes.
Just as it occurs to him that he might have heard it in his
sleep, coming from one of the spruce, smiling gravediggers
he's been talking to lately in his dreams, he sees his father
half open his mouth and move his head on the pillow; it's a
slow movement, the sort you'd expect from a body that has
forgotten its own existence, but perceptible nonetheless. He
draws near and leans toward him. Bad breath, drugs, sweat,
disinfectant: it's an effort to withstand the smell emanating
from his body. He sees him struggle to swallow and soaks
a patch of gauze in the glass of water next to the bed, then
wets his lips. His father takes a deep breath that seems almost

like a show of irritation and then sinks back into blackness. He has never seen him so pale. The skin on his face looks so thin you could tear it with a fingernail. A bruise has stained one side of his neck purple like a secret kiss. He moves a little farther away, just far enough to see his whole face, and when he's regained his focus he jumps another two steps backward, stunned. His father has opened his eyes and is looking at him. For a moment he doesn't know what to think. Has he come to? Is he dying? Then he seems to take up that lost sentence again, and the dark, moldy tongue he spoke it in; he lets out a long, dragging sound, a sort of voiced sigh that weaves through the air and then abruptly turns into a word half-way through, as though impelled by some sudden necessity, which then becomes two clear words that come together, and he speaks.

He seems to be worrying about something imminent, a danger so close and apparently so serious that it's managed to do what drugs and visitors couldn't: repatriate him after a ninety-six-hour coma, a limbo that he later—sometime during the brief interval in which his father seems to convince everybody, including the doctors, that he'll pull through—remembers with great joy, the same way many of his father's Jewish clients remember the stay at the Király thermal baths that he inserts into their itineraries without telling them, like a secret courtesy. He's very agitated. He lifts a hand and points to one side with his index finger, signaling a vague area between the terry-cloth slippers he still refuses to use and a three-legged IV stand. He asks, demands to be given his pants. He demands just like that, in general, not aiming the request at him, his son, who never has been nor ever will be as thankful for anything as for the gift of hearing his voice again after the four days he's been in a coma; it's not aimed at him, though he's fixed his gaze on him and is now separated from him by less than twenty centimeters, but at nobody, or maybe at the same unknown, hazy interlocutor he was speaking to a few minutes earlier, while he was asleep. He needs his pants, the money in the pocket of his pants, right now. He has to tip the morning nurse before she leaves. Because if he waits, who knows what the others will do with the cash? It's no use telling him that it's two in the morning, that the morning nurse won't be there for five hours, that there's no rush. He isn't listening. He tilts his head very slightly to one side with a cheerful distrust, like a dog whose master is attempting to speak its language, but nothing he hears seems to penetrate the stupor that's shielding him. Now, he wants his pants now, before the shift ends and the nurse leaves. The only nurse who speaks German. There, in the pocket. He's asking him this one favor: to get the cash from his pants pocket. His son changes tack. Maybe playing along will work better than contradicting him. How much does he want to give her? His father hesitates. He frowns, as though calculating, and while they waver, his eyes recover a little glimmer of humanity. Twenty thousand pesos? When he hears this, he laughs. The eight days his father has spent in the hospital probably cost the same amount. Twenty thousand? he repeats, you think so? His father looks at him again. I don't know, he says, thirty thousand? The nurse speaks perfect German. She's pretty, too, and she wears real shoes, not those flat pieces of junk nurses usually drag around. And she knows all the songs by heart: "Hans hat Hosen an," "Laterne, Laterne," "O Tannenbaum," "Der Kuckuck und der Esel." There, in my pants, he says, and points blindly again, and then he suddenly sticks an elbow into the bed and sits halfway up, sweeping the edges of the room with a keen, suspicious look. He leaps toward him to stop him, and while he's there he pushes the button hanging from the bed. He's so weak that his catheter and the wires connecting him to the heart monitor are enough to restrain him. He looks at himself for the first time, at his arms, and then his chest, and then he starts to follow the course of the tube emerging from his wrist but gives up after a few seconds, exhausted. All the evidence is there; none of it is powerful enough to prevail and break through to his consciousness. He sweeps the room again, looking confused. He can't see his pants. He's asking where his pants are. Blue corduroy; thick, blue corduroy. They were there, on the chair, before dinner arrived. Someone must have stolen them. He strokes his father's face, smooths the wild clumps of hair that spring up when he lifts his head from the pillow. They must have taken them away to clean them, he tells him, and offers to leave the money for the nurse himself. His father looks at him in surprise, as though he's not convinced but doesn't think the idea is so absurd as to be ruled out immediately. He takes some cash out of his pocket and shows it to his father. Tell me how much and I'll give it to her, he says. His father points to a few notes with his chin. Which, he asks him. The blue ones, says his father. How many, he says. Two, says his father: two blues. And then he seems to have second thoughts, and says, is that too much? His son smiles again.

It's less than the price of one of the two packets of cigarettes his father has smoked every day since he was thirteen years old, and twice what the nurse who responds to the bell pays for the packet of peppermint gum she buys every time she works overnight in intensive care, a well-chewed stick of which is now releasing its last languid reserves of flavor into her mouth. No, it's not dementia, it's disorientation, says the nurse, and, charged with this unexpected technical nuance, the word feels new and gleams as though he were hearing it for the first time. It's common in surgical patients who spend a long time isolated in intensive care, without the vital contact with the world—day, night, other people, the TV news—that makes it through, albeit in regulated form, to normal hospital rooms. And it's while he's in this trance, a sort of benign, candid dizziness that makes him seem like a drunk child, which can devastate and bring tears of laughter at the same time and last for hours unbroken by anyone or anything, dragging its shipwrecked subject to extremes of delirium—it's while he's in this state that his father is suddenly swept along by the topic of conversation (money: the four, five, twenty, or thirty thousand pesos he must give to the morning nurse, the only one in this pseudo-German hospital with whom he can sing German children's songs, which besides the language rotting inside him because he never speaks it to anyone any longer is the only treasure he has left of the Germany he left behind sixty-eight years earlier) and sets about digging up those ten hellish days.

It's hard to follow him. He grasps the basics: that the casualness, almost indifference with which his father told him that the money would be returned to him in stages was nothing but a bluff, a cover sustained only by an enormous effort in order to buy himself time to search for and, if he was lucky, find the pair of lowlifes in charge of the "financial operation" in which the money had supposedly ended up, twin brothers who don't answer the phone for days, or go to the extravagant offices they only use for occasional cups of coffee, checking the mail, and admiring the calves of the numerous secretaries who'll soon end up on the street. The matter gets more complicated with every day, every hour, every minute that passes, because that's how things are in the demented economy of the day: forever dividing, getting smaller and smaller until the whole weight of events is concentrated on a single point— the present—which might not withstand the pressure. He hears rumors that the twins are in Uruguay, maybe in prison, or buying land, or competing together for all they're worth in an offshore regatta; in any case very far, geographically but moreover morally, from assuming any responsibility to the investors and savers they've left behind in Buenos Aires, who spring up like fungus and can be found uselessly standing guard, squeezing homemade receipts signed by some flunky in their fists, in the bars near the office, the parking lot where the twins have left their latest-model cars, and the country houses (also twin) where they live—or used to live before the embezzlement—with their blond wives, who are tan even in the middle of winter from sun reflected on snow. It's difficult to figure out the order of events from his father's account—if *account* is the right word for the coils of memory he twines and untwines in the darkness of the intensive care unit, his eyes like saucers, like the eyes of someone who's sleepwalking or has been possessed or hypnotized; the dry, glassy eyes associated with psychotropic drugs, which always seem to be lit up from the inside—but after a while it seems that actually only one of the pair, the real brains behind the scam, has been seen in Montevideo. The other one—who's apparently as much a victim as the victims themselves, if not more so, because to the financial blow he suffers must be added the emotional damage that can be caused only by the betrayal of one's own flesh and blood—stayed in Buenos Aires, in hiding, hoping to buy himself some time and breathe a little, but ultimately intending to show his face and deal with his contractual obligations. His father exhausts his means. He leaves no contact untried, knocks on every door, spends hours by the phone. In his father's version, the characters get confused; names, nicknames, and jobs are switched and rarely return to their original positions: suddenly the fugitive twin weathering the storm in his cousin's garage has the features, bushy mustache, and vices of a former work contact of his father's, a man who gets arrested for having a secret phone line; and the methods his father uses to gather the money he owes sound too much like his schemes for doing the only thing he's trained to do, clear up the mess, a prime example being the case of the pharmaceutical company that hires him to arrange an end-of-year trip as a reward for its staff and then, pleading financial difficulties, pays him six months late for the almost ninety airfares for which his father had to pay the airline strictly on time. What's clear, in any case, is that his father rolls up his sleeves, uses some contacts he isn't proud to have, gives up certain rights in exchange for information, and finally finds the twin; and once he gets to the damp, poorly lit garage where he's set up a sort of parody of an office using a table and some plastic garden chairs and an old Bakelite phone, he hears the twin himself, in a tank top and with several days' worth of stubble, red eyelids, and the brutishness that comes from being locked away—looking just like the hostages of those armed organizations who regained their freedom fifteen years earlier—tell him the very thing he's feared since the beginning: that he doesn't have the money, that he doesn't know when he will have it, that he can't even promise he'll ever have it.

Day is beginning to break. He can tell not because of the light, which is still too weak, and which melts as soon as it hits the hospital's tinted windows, but by the buzz coming from the intensive care unit's command center, which is increasing, getting more lively and more intense: the sound of a machine warming up. It's very early in the morning, and everything blends into his father's soft voice as he lies amid his monitors, which blink impassively while in the room next door a woman with almost no hair clutches her pillow, in the throes of death, and in the one opposite a young athlete lies snoring, the covers cast aside, his heart broken to pieces. So he has to *whip up* the money—a delinquent use of the phrase he's always liked. He has to whip it up in record time, and with the utmost discretion, without him, his son, ever suspecting what's going on. In his father's confused delirium, the figure ranges between ten, three hundred and fifty, and fifty thousand dollars, the variations almost as capricious and extravagant as the origins his father claims for it in the course of his explanation (a very well-paid job he never had, the sale of a car he never owned, the redundancy payment he still dreams about, and, hidden among these fakes, the real one, the living inheritance given to his son by his mother's husband); however much it is, though, his father claws it back, a little here, a little there, diverting funds from their intended destinations, helping himself to sums that don't belong to him, delaying urgent payments. For ten days he floats between scandal and crime with his head underwater, holding his breath. If just one of his maneuvers comes to light, everything will fall apart. After a couple of days of this, there's nothing, or almost nothing, to distinguish him from the lowlife who conned him. He's lied, he's promised things he won't deliver, he's got his hands on other people's money. He still sleeps in his own bed, still bathes and changes his clothes, still walks the streets undisguised and sends his clients to Rio, New York, and Rome. But these privileges won't last long. One night he inexplicably puts off going home. He sees himself on the CCTV monitor in the window of an electrical appliance store and doesn't recognize what he sees. He lingers in a bar, and then another, and then another still, and as the hours go by the basements grow more sordid, the air fouler, and the drinks lower-grade (though it's still always neat whiskey: anything else isn't alcohol, it's a bad joke), and the only thing he can feel is nausea. Shame: a kind of cold, black lava, which someone has spilled inside him and which is filling him from head to toe and rapidly turning to stone. And all this, says his father, fixing him with wide-open, shining eyes that can't even see him any longer, all this for three hundred and fifty dollars? For a return ticket to Rio?

He's moved by his father's shame, much more than by the juggling act he discovers he performed in order to return the money he'd entrusted to him, trebled in that stunningly short period. His shame, more than the ordeal of emergencies, danger, and last-gasp efforts he had to go through. He's moved by the fact that once he'd got the money back, he kept the lengths he had to go to in order to recover it secret. But what moves him most—now that his father has closed his eyes and is once more abandoning himself to sleep, exhausted by the effort of remembering, which is as titanic an undertaking as the epic tale he lived through during those ten desperate days—is seeing him getting muddled and losing his way among numbers, precisely where he's always been a beacon. He doesn't know what day it is; he's incapable of figuring out how much time separates two events; years and dates become particles blending together blindly in chaos. Temperatures, quantities, prices: anything that can be measured or counted, which has always been his element, is now a swamp in which he trips and falls and makes a fool of himself—a fool: the nightmare he has spent his whole life avoiding at any cost. Over the next few days, he often complains of having his temperature or blood samples taken five, six times a day, which happens nowhere but in his imagination, or indignantly protests that he's only had one meal and one visitor in forty-eight hours, when the supply of food is in fact perfectly regular and his visitors so numerous that the head nurse has to step in and limit them. When he's transferred to a normal room, having for a moment convinced everyone that this long hospital stay will soon be nothing but a bad memory, he's amazed countless times to see actresses he had thought dead alive and kicking on the TV (an element that's almost as innate to him as numbers), and surprised countless more times when he asks after people long buried, TV presenters or reporters whose deaths he was among the first to tell everyone about, having always been quick with breaking showbiz news. And how many times must the famous German-speaking nurse—the only one in the whole hospital, according to his father; in fact one of four or five who regularly patrol the floor, as he verifies for himself one day when he's a little weary of the exalted picture his father ceaselessly paints of her; in any case the only one to whom his father, naturally overlooking the fact that he has delegated the task to others, contrives time and again to give money, slipping it into the pocket of her uniform when she leans over him (in his version to sing "Schlaf, Kindlein, schlaf!" to him; in hers to give him a pill or change his dressing)—how many times must she beckon to him discreetly from the door to the room, so that his father won't notice, and, seeming touched but uncomfortable, as though she's just endured the lascivious advances of an elementary school student, return to him the few measly coins or the exorbitant sum his father has slipped her as a tip without her noticing.

It all disappears so quickly, anyway, swallowed by the hunger of the present moment. One year later there's nothing, not a penny left of that money, the modest capital his father saves from depreciation—recklessly or not, it doesn't matter anymore—by entering it into the Russian roulette of financial speculation, and which he himself immediately changes into dollars, on his father's advice. It's devoured by the construction work, inflation, the fees charged by the architect—who slams the door on his way out the day he gets his last payment, disappointed that he hasn't received the compensation he'd expected, and shatters the stained-glass window by the front door, his proudest addition to the house. Still, he has a house, a splendid house, his first. And when he's struck by nostalgia and he misses having cash, misses banknotes and their comforting readiness to serve, he often consoles himself by telling himself that no, he hasn't lost it, the money just looks different now, and it can be changed back to its previous form whenever he wants.

Two months after they move in, when he's been terrified by the amount of water that accumulates in the roof's covered gutters after forty-eight hours of torrential rain, eventually soaking through the ceiling and falling into the bedroom in a cascade, directly onto the lamb's wool slippers he puts on every morning of the year, summer and winter alike, he follows in the architect's footsteps and disappears. He leaves the apartment and never comes back. For a while his ex-wife vegetates in her nightdress in the still uninhabited living room, in shock. Later, thinking less of the house than his toiletry bag, his clothes, his books, his music, and the piles and piles of videotapes he's left in the top room, which he never comes back to fetch, she quickly finds a buyer, sells the house off cheaply, and gives him his half. Minus costs and extras, it's roughly the same amount in dollars that his mother's husband gave him a year and a half earlier. The famous wad of a hundred hundred-dollar bills. It's magic: eighteen months obliterated at a stroke, as if nothing had ever happened. He looks at these crisp, new, identical notes, and can't believe it; he asks himself if they're *the same ones*. There's no doubt about it: money doesn't change. This is one of its secret, miraculous laws. Everything else does, though. Him, for a start: he's older, more abject, more cowardly. And just like every other time he decides to be single again—returning to the damp but always welcoming darkness that he knows so well, which though it soon becomes suffocating he comes back to at intervals, hopelessly and as hungrily as an addict or an orphan—he realizes that if there's one person he can depend on, it's his father. And so he goes to the travel agency, puts the wad of dollars on his desk, and asks him to put together a tailor-made trip to Europe. And with that, the money vanishes, is translated once more: countries, cathedrals, crappy hotels, a coat for the rain. He comes back sick and fatter, with a cracked molar (a rogue falafel full of unidentified hard bits), tendonitis in his right ankle (from weeks of walking on the edge of his foot to keep the holey sole of his shoe off the rainy European sidewalks), and no clothes (his suitcase having been stranded in baggage purgatory).

He's pitiful. If he even had as much financial sense as a *clochard*. He spends a good part of his stay in Paris watching them, at first tenderly and then consumed by uncontrollable envy. His favorites: the one who installs himself with his bottle of wine and his newspapers in one of the glazed public phone booths that nobody uses anymore and whose doors it's almost impossible to open without dislocating a shoulder; the one who patrols the block barefoot in the middle of winter, periodically giving out an alarmed or threatening shout that nobody understands; the one who sleeps on a stairway landing at the metro station, protected by her retinue of dogs. He never gives them money. It's not that he doesn't have any—although it's the end of his trip and he's treasuring his last handful of traveler's checks as devotedly as if they were undiscovered works of art. He doesn't know how to approach them, what to say to them, how to behave as he drops a coin in their hat or dented aluminum bowl. He doesn't want to insult them. He watches them counting their donations and is moved to tears by the rapt care with which they examine and classify the coins, putting some in a pocket and keeping others—the ones they'll have to use soon—in the palm of a blackened hand. And when he gets back, he's as dirty as they are, and just as asocial and indifferent, only what in them is distance and dandyism is, in him, pure desperation.

How could he knock on his mother's door in this state? And what would he wear? The ridiculous tattered sheepskin coat he hasn't taken off since he got off the plane, even though it hasn't been in style for more than ten years and it's the middle of summer in Buenos Aires? And besides, he wouldn't find her even if he did go to her place. She's on the Uruguayan coast, half on vacation, half busy with the Beast, which already has two floors (not one, as stated in the

plans), four bedrooms (not two), two small sea-facing ter-
races (not one), and a kidney-shaped swimming pool that
takes up nearly all the space originally set aside for a garden
complete with a little gazebo and flower beds, a tribute to
the mansion in Mar del Plata that his mother's husband has
to scale down to two or three consolatory vases full of hydrangeas and relocate to one of the numerous halls that have
recently sprouted from the project. Listening to her describe
its growth over the phone, he can't tell whether his mother
is talking about a house or a living organism that's obedient
only to its own rules. It's all excitement and alarm, and the
call constantly threatens to cut out. Expenses, cash, bills, and
more bills: a bottomless pit, which, incidentally, he knows
about all too well—but the house is splendid, a strange green
cube that imposes a certain rigor on a landscape colonized by
chalet kitsch. No, he tells her: he won't go see her right now—
however much he'd like to catch the architect red-handed, expose him once and for all; he's always suspected the worst of
him, and particularly since discovering that he makes his living as a professional rugby coach and only dusts off his degree
certificate when his mother and her husband, who meet him
at a party, confess to him that they've finally decided to do
something with the four hillside plots they own. He would go,
but he's only just got back to Buenos Aires and he has to sort
everything out, find a job of some kind. Europe's expensive,
he doesn't have much money left—and then he's interrupted
by a volley of maternal laughter. "What's the problem?" she
says: "Give it to your father, he'll put it to work for you!"

It's strange. His love life falls apart in the space of a few
months, and he doesn't shed a single tear. Until the day he
goes to the bank to close the safe deposit box he used to share
with his ex-wife (box two, unit three), which in fact he still
shares, as demonstrated by the two matching keys he gives
back and her signature below his on the record card like a

miniature electrocardiogram. They go in, through two slid-
ing, prisonlike grille doors, and when the woman who works
for the bank asks him to open the metal box to confirm that
it's empty, a necessary stage in the process of giving it up, his
knees suddenly go weak, and he only avoids falling over by
putting a hand on the woman's delicate shoulder while she
looks at him in consternation. Sitting on the edge of the seat
that's hurriedly brought to him—one of the high, uncomfortable stools he sometimes used to sit on while depositing or
withdrawing something from the box, whenever he found
himself suddenly drawn to the two tiny, red, padded chests
that appeared at the bottom, and opened them and sat for a
while contemplating the modest, slightly childlike beauty of
the two pieces of jewelry his ex-wife loved like nothing else in
the world—sitting there on the stool, he starts crying openly
and at length, and noisily, howling like a beaten animal, and
his tears fall and hit the bottom of the empty box and shatter
into a thousand microscopic shards, a thousand watery diamonds that belong to him, that in fact *are* him, but which will
stay there forever, locked away in that little flattened coffin.

Closing the account is even more agonizing, and he has to
come back several times. There's a missing signature, he forgets his ID, he's just been sent some money that hasn't been
credited to the account yet. Every time he pushes the glass
door open and walks into the bank, he feels his chest contract
in a spasm of pain. It doesn't surprise him the first time, when
he sits opposite the account manager he's been seeing forever
and tells her that he's decided to close the account, and after
listening to the full repertoire of possible alternatives with
which she tries to change his mind—all of them written in
angry red in her client-retention manual, and all formulated
with equally suspicious clarity and benevolence—he hears his
voice faltering and finds himself confessing the only thing he
promised himself he wouldn't admit even under torture: that

they've split up, that it doesn't make sense to have a shared account any longer. The next visits are more difficult. And yet the bank isn't the first crime scene he's returned to. He's drunk in the bars he used to meet his ex-wife in and smoked in the cold in the forbidding square where he grabbed her and kissed her against a tree, inexcusably grazing her elbows on the bark. He's already been caught alone and with his guard down by songs they used to listen to together, friends used to seeing them together, smells or urges that only make sense, that he'd only smell or pursue if he were with her. He's not indifferent to any of these blows, but their effect never amounts to more than an agreeable sense of déjà vu, like something you'd experience in a museum of romance; they're more like souvenirs or a form of preservation than stones sent from the beyond to chip the glass cube in which he's trying to catch his breath. The impersonal atmosphere of the bank, on the other hand, the fluorescent strip lighting, the dirty upholstery on the seats, and the employees' uniforms, which always fit badly and are covered in stray threads, not to mention the condescension they've always treated him with (given how insignificant a client he is), the lines he's forced to stand in, the number of times he's called without anybody answering, and the silent, daily swindle they subject him to: all of the most insipid and abhorrent elements of this place they seldom visited together ("Everybody should go to a bank at least once in their life. To rob it," she liked to quote, blowing the smoke from an invisible 1873 Colt Peacemaker), and which he's come back to now to take his leave, come together and suddenly form a world, a kind of unique, poisonous, palpable atmosphere, and mere contact with it is enough to expose him, the imperturbable man, to the elements, leaving him so defenseless that the faintest evocation of his former life could kill him.

He's waiting in line one afternoon, probably for the last

time, holding the handful of signed, sealed documents that will set him free—at least from this bank, or from this branch, or from this love that he so underestimated. He's brought something to read. He likes the shield of arrogant indifference a book erects between him and the world, especially when he senses a queue agitator nearby, the type of person that sighs, raises their weary eyes to the ceiling, complains, seeks complicity, wishes the most hellish punishments on the bank and its employees, and when it's their turn stands in front of the window and slides their check or their bill forward as politely as a geisha. He's reading, or rather indolently skating over, a page with the right corner folded down—a sign that this isn't the first time he's paused on it in passing—on which a young disciple whose abilities have abandoned him announces his own radical powerlessness and surrenders before his master, thanking him for everything he's done for him, everything he's given to him, and the truths he's enabled him to understand, but asking him to forget him forever, when the line advances two spaces and the back of a gleaming head of straight, jet-black hair—which from his position three people back he assumes is a wig—appears in front of the window, and the employee serving it checks something on a card and then raises her eyes toward it and forms the fateful phrase he never imagined he'd hear, the only one he should have expected to hear: "Box two, unit three." *His* box, with *his* emptiness and *his* tears trapped inside.

She's wearing blue boat shoes with no socks. The ankle of one leg scratches the calf of the other, with the absentminded aptitude with which certain parts of the body do things without informing the rest. He decides to follow her. He doesn't even have to think about it. He attends to everything else—the closure of the account and the last pesos they steal from him, which he pays impatiently, without saying a word, before just as impatiently squeezing the indifferent hand that's presented to him through the hole in the window by way of goodbye—judiciously and imperceptibly, in a hazy background like the ones in which sleepwalkers carry out their simulations of gestures. He looks for the woman, wondering which of the bank's secret folds must have swallowed her, and then sees her walking toward the door that leads to the safe deposit boxes. The buzzer sounds. The woman struggles with the door for a few seconds (seconds that he could use to go over and relay the secrets he no longer needs: the light yank toward yourself and subsequent push that open it) and then disappears to the other side. It's like he can see her, like he's already watching her on one of the security cameras that will be installed a few years later, before whose unsleeping eye the successors of the employee who served him will open other clients' safe deposit boxes in order to prove before a third party, and before nobody, that they're empty. He knows exactly what she'll do in there. He knows how long she'll spend isolated from the world, unassailable, her very being momentarily transformed into wealth; how long it will take her to pass through the bars, unlock the door to the unit, take out the elongated coffin, put her treasures inside, slot the box back in, sign the paperwork, and leave. And when she leaves, he's waiting for her outside, looking inattentively at the window display of the bookshop next door. By now, there are no prices: values change so rapidly that booksellers have stopped trying to keep up.

Five months later, he reappears in the same frame—the bookshop window (now with other books in it, priced in pesos rather than australs, because there are now ten thousand australs to the peso) and the same slice of the bank's façade with its red granite column and the pane of a glass door with a spray can's insulting stamp on it—with shorter hair, an anachronistic mustache that would be at home on a seventies porn star, and an elegant navy-blue wool duffle coat in place of the old sheepskin one. He goes into the bank, stands in front of the cashier's window, and, showing no sign of emotion, says, "Box two, unit three." As he tells his father, who follows his romantic adventures with a vague interest that's too halfhearted to outlast the surprise of novelty, it's possible that he followed her, approached her, and finally, after a quiet and tenacious courtship, made her fall in love with him for this purpose alone, because he's obsessed by the metal coffin she's unwittingly inherited from him and wants to be able to say, once more, the four words of banking jargon that designate it, or simply because he can't bear the idea of having to stop saying them. This is what relationship experts call a connection, a word that casts as a romantic miracle something that in truth isn't much more than a phenomenon of mechanical compensation, not fundamentally very different from those involving a long-sighted eye and the lens that corrects it, or a wooden platform that lengthens a short leg just the right amount. He's in the game again. Will he be able to do it? His heiress—as he privately thinks of her, feeling the secret joy of a creditor mentally delighting in the obliviousness of a debtor who doesn't yet know quite how much he owes—is forty-two, the wife of a playwright or a screenwriter or a folk lyricist, in any case a successful man endowed with the bad taste to die during a trip to the interior of the country (after a cow looking for something to graze on in the night cuts him off in the middle of the road); with the courtesy not to forget the relatives he leaves behind, to whom he periodically sends money from the beyond (as playwrights, screenwriters, and lyricists call their royalty payments); and with an intractable son with an acne-strewn face, who wears clothes two sizes too large, abhors his father's literary heritage with all his heart despite never having read it ("What for, if I abhor him with all my heart?"), and is pretty much at war with the world, Sonia, the widow, and her Prince Valiant haircut. A fixation that dates to time immemorial: she already has it in the uniformly blurry photos of her fifteenth birthday party. And no, it's not a wig, as he is suitably disappointed to discover the first time he holds the nape of her neck and draws her head toward him to kiss her, standing in the bright galley kitchen of what will soon, very soon, be his new home, a few seconds after the bulb shatters almost on top of their heads, throwing a veil of darkness on the encounter, and a few before the teenage vandal bursts in on his skates, only just avoiding knocking them into the papered wall.

This type of attack is common currency in the early days. The boy leaves him waiting, hangs up the phone, doesn't pass on his messages. He tells him that Sonia isn't home (when she's just poured herself a glass of wine to wait for him), that she doesn't want to see him (when she's just put on perfume for him), that he'll never set foot in the house again (when he already has two pairs of shoes in the closet). The bottle of champagne he brings (which he drives himself crazy looking for) shows up two days later among the cleaning things in one of the kitchen cupboards, empty, of course, and the tub of ice cream in the bottom drawer of his father's desk, leaking its multicolored juices on the original manuscript of *Danger*, the oratorio the dramaturge was writing when he embedded the front of his Honda Civic in that cow's flabby flank. After an unexpectedly passionate soiree on the couch, he finds chewing gum stuck in the buttonholes of his sheepskin coat. When he goes home and tries to open his door, he discovers that he doesn't have his keys—the boy is at that moment using them to remove an antediluvian mat of hair and semen from the drain in the bathtub. He doesn't allow it to intimidate him. He only has to see how the delinquent treats the supermarket delivery boy, the guy at the video store, and his guitar teacher to realize that it's not personal, even if the delivery boy, the video store guy, and the guitar teacher don't also get the accusations he shouts at the top of his lungs, seeming as though he's on the verge of a fit, like some sort of epileptic Hamlet, of aspiring to a throne that isn't rightfully theirs. Where does he—he, in whose eyes any new situation tends to look like evil and danger—find his lion tamer's levelheadedness and strange detachment? Something makes him immune to this type of rage, something even he didn't know he had, and like any lucky weapon—as he learns very early on thanks to the chapters of his superhero comics that reveal how the superheroes discovered their powers—it's doubly effective because it's power in its purest form, used without control or calculation. Little by little—like someone realizing that the dreams he's been having, his ideas, the things he buys, the rituals he surrenders himself to, all of these signs, though they're scattered in time and space, in fact constitute just one thing, one crucial need, to which from that moment on he will unhesitatingly sacrifice his life if necessary—he discovers that he likes being where he is now, *in the middle*, in neither a central position, like a lover barging into a wake and abducting the widow while she's still warm from sobbing, nor a subordinate one, like a slave offering his services as compensation for her grief. In fact, he's the one who intercepts the homemade ammunition of rolled-up bread filled with coins that the boy cheerfully fires at his mother, using his body as a shield. And he's the one who holds talks with the hooligan when he shuts himself in his room. He comes and goes, gives and takes, announces and relays. And for once, luck is on his side. One afternoon, in one of the neighborhoods full of low-rise houses that still exist in Buenos Aires, he stumbles upon a near-deserted pharmacy and spies a bar of the astringent soap he used to stop an untimely bout of acne when he was twenty-six, sitting helplessly in one of its dusty windows like the star of a very old film that was never released. He goes in, buys every bar they have—so that the scent of sulfur intoxicates him on the way home—and promises to give one to the boy if he doesn't follow through with his threat to make a bonfire of his clothes in the middle of his bedroom. The boy accepts. Three days later, his cheeks and the spot between his eyebrows—formerly no-man's-lands ravaged by the sebum's troops—are clean, soft, and smooth, and that night the boy comes home making out with a girlfriend of sorts. One night while they're eating together (if *eat* is the right word for this slow, phlegmatic dissection of two eggplants parmesan), the boy asks permission to leave the table and isn't given it, but as usual leaves anyway, dropping his napkin and showering the floor with breadcrumbs. Sonia sobs and dries her tears with a somewhat dirty napkin, and he consoles her and ends up sitting next to her, on her seat, both of them uncomfortable, while the eggplant that's been left half-eaten because of her tears turns to liquid. At some point he gets up and goes to the bathroom, and on the way he catches the boy in his mother's room, stealing money from her purse. He's about to walk on by without saying anything, but suddenly he stands still and looks straight at him until the boy stops counting notes and looks back at him, startled.

But what he's interested in is the box, the safe deposit box, going to the bank every now and then and saying, "Box two, unit three," and putting the key in the lock—the same lock he used in his former life, with the classic difficulty of never remembering which way to insert the key, whether the teeth should be facing right or left—and then taking it out, opening it, and seeking refuge in it under that intrusive gaze before tenderly filling it with all the things Sonia has asked him to store: jewels, bonds, deeds, foreign currency. This is it, this ridiculous, solitary ceremony that sometimes draws a few tears from him and leaves him feeling exhausted, as though he's emerging from an emotional ordeal; this and not the money, despite the gigolo hypothesis his mother reproaches him with when he fills her in on the new developments in his life. "Wasn't living off women always one of your secret fantasies?" she says, smiling from ear to ear, a little buzzed after a visit to the osteopath. As far as he's aware, there's no key to the nerve center of his secret fantasies, and if there is one, his mother has never had a copy, unless all mothers by law, by virtue of being mothers, have a direct line to the laboratories where their children's secret fantasies are cooked up. *He*'s never given her one, anyway. How she arrives at this idea, where she plucks it from, and above all where she gets her conviction are not things he's currently in a position to know. Maybe later, when the black hole of the Beast has devoured everything—money, other properties, savings, credit, even itself—and ruined her completely, and she doubles her stakes—his mother, who her whole life has barely even played the lottery, and who even then always banks on losing as little as possible by buying the cheapest ticket—and decides, at the age of sixty, to give up the only thing she has left, thirty-five years of marriage, and to go live alone in an apartment that at forty-five square meters is smaller than one of the en-suite bathrooms the ex-rugby-guy-turned-architect had the bright idea of installing in the Beast, and to resume the studies in translation that she abandoned almost as soon as she'd begun them, when she found herself alone, with a child, and chose to get married again so as not to fall back into the hellish web of her own family.

It's not the money; it's the box (two), the object itself, which he always removes from the unit (three) as carefully and solemnly as an undertaker taking a niche out of a tomb. The box is his own death, his only possible counter or balance to the terrible void left in this woman and this boy by the successful dramatist when he dazzled that cow in the middle of the road (the police report notes that he was driving with his high beams on) and then plowed into it. (And what a

relief it is, what a pleasure, almost, to literally occupy someone else's place, his warm impression in the bed, his hangers
in the wardrobe, the head of the table!) The box is his treasure, his secret fetish, his passion. If his life were a depraved
film—one of those dark, melancholic curios whose sole purpose (to awaken the unmistakable tingling that reminds the
crotch of its own existence) is hidden behind a catalog of tortuous clinical syndromes, just like an old compendium of
sexual psychopathy—if this were such a film, his alter ego—
probably older and balder, with gnawed fingernails, dandruff
on his shoulders, and the cuff of one of his pant legs trailing
on the floor—would tremble more than he does when he puts
the key in the lock; he'd bite his lip a little as he withdrew the
box and squeeze it to his body as he took it to the cubicle,
as though stealing it or trying to suffocate it with the heat
of his desire, and once in the cubicle, after taking the cover
off with his greedy eyes wide open and standing in front of
it with his stool jamming the door shut, he'd relieve himself
until he passed out, depositing something money can't buy,
something nobody would ever think to steal, either because
it's worth nothing or because it's of incalculable value. Not
him. If he leaves anything in the box when he goes to the
bank—other than what Sonia asks him to put in there, that
is—it's not drops of his pitiful life force, which he strangles
with a slippery knot in the latex sheaths where they go to
die two or three times a week, preferably in the morning. It's
knickknacks, things of no great value, personal effects that
wouldn't grab anyone's attention if they were brought out
into the light or placed in plain view on a dresser or a book-
shelf: a notebook (his dream diary), a medal from the only
chess tournament he ever competed in (he came in third, but
he was barely sixteen, and the winner, whom he backed into
a corner for the duration of their game but didn't find a way
to finish off, a worldly fifty), an envelope containing pictures

from his childhood (beach, beach with a sausage dog, beach with his grandmother and the sausage dog), a die (which once rolled and landed on six, giving him his only ever five-of-a-kind), a green frog with black stripes, sky-blue brushstrokes, and disproportionately large eyes, made of tin and attached to a string, which releases the few remaining twists on its windup key and starts jumping around like crazy as soon as he closes the lid, as though it were fighting not to be buried alive among those title deeds, wads of pounds sterling, and pearl necklaces in velvet boxes.

Technically—which is how his mother always discusses the matter—he does live off the widow, of course. But it all happens so fluidly and so naturally that he never even has time to feel any shame about it. He's given access to every-thing, bank accounts and checkbooks, his name is added to credit cards, even fixed-term deposits and investments are open to him, though these being provinces of the world of money that he has no idea what to do with, he sticks to car-rying out orders. He's frugal, much more frugal now that he "has money" (his mother's quote marks) than he was when his money was really his, or when he didn't have any. His mother can't bear it. For example: they meet for lunch. His mother, an amateur gourmet, has picked the dining room of a former convent in the middle of the business district, a territory into which she sometimes ventures with purely provocative intentions, to challenge her son's comfort in his assumption that the neighborhood has one owner and that owner is his father. While she loses herself in the menu amid sighs of pleasure, as tempted by the monastic selection of dishes as a moth by a flickering light, he unfolds his napkin with a vaguely magician-like gesture, without so much as looking at the menu, and orders a plate of mixed vegetables, or a boiled potato with olive oil, or some white rice. "Enough, you fraud," his mother rebukes him, snapping her menu closed so that it releases a silent explosion: "Don't pretend to be some kind of fakir; your widow isn't watching you; order something decent." He pays, as he's always done. But when did "always" start? And why? And who decided on this arrangement, if he, its primary victim, can't remember agreeing on anything with anyone, try as he may? Maybe if he thinks harder . . . The change. Ah, the change! Maybe this agreement is nothing but the continuation by other means—the "higher stage," in the words of the older brother of the only friend he successfully drags to the Communist Party cinema, an enterprising Trotskyist who uses the lowest, most extortionate means (photos of Leon Davidovich's skull split open by Ramón Mercader's ice pick, among other things) to extract a monthly membership fee from him for a year and a half, telling him it goes toward funding the party's journal—of his old, proverbial role as lender of emergency small change. Maybe.

For the time being, he doesn't argue. He's too intrigued by his mother's interest in his romantic situation. By this eagerness, which is made up of suspicion and rivalry at once . . . By this strange anticipation . . . The last time he remembers experiencing anything similar, he's sixteen years old and has just started going out with an extraordinarily earnest girlfriend, a militant member of a leftist youth group who never reads books of fewer than six hundred pages, has a perfect instinct for gifts (a pair of flippers, a telescope, a fountain pen that will last him twenty-two years), and visits him with businesslike regularity every time he gets sick. The moment his mother leaves them alone, she shoots a disapproving look at his box of antibiotics and, with one of her two-lipped magic tricks—kissing, indoctrinating: which comes first?—tries to convert him to the dogma of homeopathy. "I know you're not going to like what I'm about to say, but I'm going to say it anyway," his mother tells him that night, moments after his wonder girlfriend leaves, not before gathering a heap of snotty tissues with surprising fortitude and throwing them in the trash. "Don't even think about marrying that girl. Listen to me: live a little first, then get married." After that, there's nothing, not a single word either for or against, never anything more on the subject, and with good reason: she must become immune to such worries when he doesn't pay any attention, either then, in the case of the precocious Bolshevik Florence Nightingale, with whom he ends up moving in and spending nearly ten years afloat in a voluptuous, feverish world, or the next time, with the musical therapist, or ever. And when he succumbs to his last love, the one that falls apart over the same eleven months it takes to finish the house that's supposed to shelter it, she's so preoccupied, so absorbed by the crazed progress of the Beast, that she doesn't even remember to give him the reed blinds she promised him for the gallery. And yet the widow obviously interests her. She's very careful not to show it, as though asking about her directly would be a sign of weakness or an admission of defeat. But her attention to the changes that spring up in him betrays her. Nothing escapes her. She notices when he wears a shirt in an unexpected color, or slips in a new word that's still a little rigid and crisp in the sentence, like new sheets, or absorbs and neutralizes her anxiety attacks effortlessly and with a show of good humor, though they used to infuriate him, and every time all of her alarm bells go off at once, mobilizing her legion of molecular spies around the only foreign body liable to have inspired these developments. Sometimes she interprets the delinquent's behavior as a sign. Maybe it entertains her to see her son dealing with a misfit of the type he never was at that age; whatever the reason, whenever he relays the stories of his crimes to her—in minute detail, as though trying to underscore the difference between the nightmare he's suffering as an innocent, utterly unsuspecting substitute father and the heavenly, low-key child she once had—she so rejoices in hearing them that the perfectly irrelevant advice she insists on repaying him with afterward, while she's still trembling with laughter, sounds to him like disguised arguments for the defense. In any case, while she pieces together the widow's personality from the bottle-green shirt he shows up in, the new haircut that suddenly makes him seem like a child, and the chivalrous impulses he lavishes upon her, she also builds a mental picture of it based on the boy's misdeeds—without, of course, ever revealing to him the identikit she's assembled, a freakish cameo that's part manipulative harpy, part passive-aggressive monster, in line with the jargon of the psychological parish of which she's been a devotee for decades, with the most counterproductive results.

All this changes nothing for him. Since that first time, when he ignored her objection to his Bolshevik girlfriend, his love life has unfolded far away from his mother, on another plane; it's not shielded—since it's not protected by anything too visible—so much as stubborn and invulnerable, protected by its own rules and protocols, like the tax havens that are becoming fashionable at around the same time, which are generally to be found on more or less remote islands, hermetic protectorates, tiny countries that are weak at first glance but have the unique strength of discretion, the ability to hoard secrets that the rest of the world goes out of its way to find out. He's brought the whole system to such a state of perfection that nowadays he doesn't even have to worry about safeguarding any information. He's not afraid. He could tell her anything—and in fact he does, not only when he admits that his bottle-green shirt, old-fashioned manners, and short hair are the direct result of Sonia's wishes, but also explicitly, when he describes her appearance (and has some difficulty explaining the concept of a Prince Valiant haircut, owing to his mother's gross ignorance in the matter of comics) or her moral character (she gives money to everyone who asks her on the street, every time, without exception or justification, and she removes anyone who has a live-in maid from her social circle), or when he divulges her habits (an hour of yoga between morning sex and breakfast, limited TV, windows wide open in the middle of winter)—and the secret would still be right there, intact, inaccessible to his mother, like openly transmitted frequencies that are audible only to highly trained ears. One day while he's waiting for her at the only serviceable table in the patisserie she's arranged to meet him in—one of the unpredictable spots to which his mother is faithful to the point of fanaticism, simply because they offer her something she can't resist, just one thing, something unusual but not necessarily indispensable, like two-ply toilet paper in the ladies' restroom, for example, or white, pure-cotton tablecloths, or Renaissance music, or the sickly sweet whiskey liqueur on which she gets hooked on the ferry that takes her to the Beast—he starts to look through some photos he's just had developed, souvenirs from a "getaway"—one of the widowisms most likely to raise his mother's hackles—to Misiones, which starts badly, on a precarious dinghy at Iguazú Falls that the delinquent, who's been averse to lifejackets since childhood, threatens to slash with the Victorinox he convinced his mother to buy him from the shop in the hotel's lobby, and ends worse, in a cell at the police station on the Triple Frontier, where he spends six hours in an animated trilingual conclave (Brazilian prostitute, Argentine dealer, Paraguayan smuggler), having been accused of screening a *pornochanchada* on twenty-five color TVs at an electrical appliance store in Foz de Iguazú. He's wondering for the nth time why what he sees in the viewfinder when he takes a photo is never the same color as the nine-by-thirteen prints that are supposed to capture it, why, for God's sake, he can now see things he thought he'd left out of the frame (the back of a yellow Renault 12;

the hand—index finger extended, wrist covered in fake gold watches—of the tourist from Minas Gerais who hounded them with his affability and his bad breath), but not, though he searches desperately and even considers going back to the photo lab to complain, things he was sure he'd caught (the smiling, sleeping widow's slightly aquiline profile on her pillow), when his mother arrives and stands by his side, looking down at the photos as he goes through them, and after savoring a few flashes of banal intimacy—the widow wearing her bathing suit, a poolside massage, eating breakfast on the balcony in a robe, dazzled outside the toucan enclosure at the bird sanctuary, smiling on her pillow, sleeping with her mouth half open—she sits down, takes off her sunglasses with a trembling hand, and says: "How can you take such ugly pictures? Isn't it time you got yourself a decent camera?" No, he's not afraid to tell and show her everything, because he knows that entrusting the secret to his mother, offering it up like this, freely, to her foolishness, is the best way to keep it.

But if his mother disdains his photos, that's only because it's a different secret that keeps her up at night; one that won't be found in those stupid, poorly composed pictures, but elsewhere: encrypted in bank statements, in the sums of money that arrive to enlarge them every three months with Swiss regularity, even though nobody's lifted a finger to bring them into existence. *The money of the dead.* This is what drives her crazy, and he knows it: Isn't it what drives him crazy, too? Could there be a better, more perfect type of money? Cash that falls from the sky, that rains down of its own accord, without anyone winning it or taking the trouble to send it or claiming it; pure, beneficent cash from the beyond, as impersonal as the seasons, blossom, the tide. They share this unutterable envy, an envy from which there's no solace and which reaches almost criminal heights in his mother—who, as a young woman, in a moment of harebrained inspiration during the stupefied interval between her two husbands, conceived a plan to seduce a jazz trumpeter, an affectionate, smooth-chinned guy, on the autism spectrum but extraordinarily prolific and capable of composing three flawless standards in the time it takes a taxi to drive him to the family company where he's made to earn his keep. It's awoken in them by the beneficiaries of rights and royalties, privileged creatures who are superior to any aristocrat or well-to-do bourgeois, and above all superior to the piranhas that make their killings on the money market: inventors and their children, authors and their descendants, the heirs of visionaries who had one idea and put it into action and sent it around the world, so that from then on it was the idea and not them, the visionaries, with their sweat, their tears, and their blood, whose existence would be dedicated to making money.

"Why?" his mother shouts (having put her sunglasses back on, as she does every time she suffers an attack of emotion) while reaching across the table, setting the bottle of oil swaying, and shaking him by the lapels of his tweed jacket—Sonia's latest addition to his wardrobe. "Why the hell weren't you an author? Why weren't you a genius, a writer, a scientist, one of those precocious, sickly musicians who die young, before they've met a woman or had children, and leave the rights to all their work to their mothers?" If she talks with such fury and grief now, while she's still enjoying the money from *her* dead people and all she has to do is wake up with an idea one morning and translate that money into whichever language she likes (it having already been translated from the package her father leaves her when he dies, when, yes, he's an old man, but more significantly he's full of poisonous rancor after submitting to half a dozen unsuccessful cataract operations, and is almost blind but still sufficiently clear-sighted to realize before he dies that everything he's leaving, the steel factory in Villa Devoto, the apartment in Belgrano R, the chalet in Miramar, the two cars, will be lost entirely, that in truth he's leaving it to ruin and disaster), whether she wants to translate it into things, possessions, journeys, even ambitious undertakings like the Beast, which is initially just one of many investments that claim her dead relatives' money, and then soon enough the main one and then the only one, so thoroughly does the project that starts as a summerhouse and ends up as a mansion-mausoleum, a palatial catastrophe, end up devouring everything she has, including money in the bank, of course, and also the apartment in Belgrano R, the chalet in Miramar, et cetera—if she talks like this now, while she's still swimming in money, as the phrase has it, what will she say in seven, eight years' time, when there isn't a single drop of water left in the pool, when not much more remains of her dead relatives' money than of everything else she's managed to preserve of them—dust-encrusted fossils, vague memories, the distorted echo of a voice babbling nonsense in the dark.

Yes, inheriting has its appeal. As a former heir, an unborn heir, an heir who's dead on arrival and whose calling is to wait for something that will never come to pass, he knows this firsthand. He knows the impatience, the unhealthy hunger, and the arrogance of those who know it's only a matter of time. *Sooner or later*: the heir's motto, the phrase every heir repeats at night as a talisman to calm the nerves before sleep, at the end of humbling days that demand now, immediately, what they still don't have, what a heart attack, cancer, or a drunk bottle-truck driver turning a corner at full speed will someday give them—sooner or later. An heir's laugh is acid and deafening. It's the laugh of he who laughs last, a cackle of resentment and long-brewed vengeance that leaves nobody unscathed. But if only that were all there was to it. Because even inheriting carries a responsibility. You have to live up to an inheritance. If his mother gives in to the widow's pull

on her despite her natural reserve and the armor-plating provided by her pride, it's because she realizes how much further
this other woman has managed to go. Compared with the
miracle she's pulled off—money that periodically *falls from
the sky*, gusts of cash that blow in like the wind, renewing
themselves constantly and inexhaustibly, like letters written
in death by her besotted folklorist, when his love has been
immortalized in the same formaldehyde solution that stops
his body from decomposing—compared with this, inheriting
seems like a flawed model, one of the many ingenious ideas
reduced to nothing but a pathetic, throwaway draft by haste,
greed, or ineptitude, or a fateful combination of the three.

And besides, his mother has already received her inheritance, as has her husband, and every legal heir—anyone
whose life has at some point been tethered to an inheritance,
has pulsed in the shade of its promise; who's been held in
suspense, waiting eternally and reaching for a future that will
surely grant them what's theirs once and for all—realizes,
after they inherit, the extent to which those earlier days are
mortgaged against the euphoria they feel on becoming rich.
And once the inheritance is theirs, all that remains is the fatal process of its erosion, be it abrupt or gradual, careful or
crazed. His mother and her husband understood this well—
too well, judging by the speed with which they embarked on
the wealth-liquidation program of which the Beast was really
less the cause than the prime example.

In just over five years, this imposing cuboid, which breaks
through the trees like a concrete bunker as soon as you clear
the bend in the road leading up the hill, ceases to be the he-
donistic haven it was intended to be—and which it actually
is, at least in the early days, while his mother and her husband and some close friends, all of them equally under the
ex-rugby-guy-turned-architect's inexplicable spell, still find
the house's exaggerated dimensions appealingly eccentric, a

luxury to be explored, and, like children setting about occupying a mansion recently vacated by their parents, sleep in one wing one night and another the next, eat dinner scattered among the various dining rooms, shower in a different bathroom every day, bump into one another while wandering the hallways, and set up camp on beach recliners in the deserted playrooms with their glasses of wine and their Mel Tormé and Tony Bennett records—and becomes a worry. There's no less accurate definition, nothing more deceptive than describing a house as an "immovable good," especially when it's been built from scratch. People think that once the last baseboard has been put in, the last lampshade attached, the last screw tightened on the last doorknob, that's that: the house doesn't require anything more; it's time for everyone else, the people who'll be living in it, to take their turn now. After the Beast, his mother won't stand for anyone repeating this fallacy. It's the other way around. It's not until a house is finished that it really begins to live, to need, to demand. That's when its true, living, animal nature emerges. But by then it's too late.

Every time they leave, tan and feeling the contented exhaustion and strange expert youthfulness that six weeks of sea and leisure work on their bodies, and she turns around in the car and sees the house receding and being swallowed by the trees again, like a film shown in reverse, she has the unsettling feeling that she's leaving a precious gem out in the open, unprotected and at the mercy of whoever finds it first. This feeling, along with a few robberies in the area, convinces them to hire house sitters. A Uruguayan woman who lives in the neighborhood advises them to look for a couple (since single male house sitters tend to slovenliness and alcohol, especially in the winter, when the only living beings prowling the area are stray dogs and toothless old hippies who've lost their way), and tells his mother's husband he should employ them legally, paying all the necessary taxes and insurance, more because of the risk of inspection than out of any particular commitment to social ethics. Three months later, after a decidedly unrigorous interview process that his mother and her husband use primarily as an excuse to escape Buenos Aires, a jovial sort of family—in the stifled, Uruguayan vein of joviality, and with two antisocial but hyperactive kids—moves into the ground floor of the Beast, where they will live for almost a decade as taciturn witnesses to a decadence to which they never draw attention, no doubt because they fear that the first step toward curbing it would be to fire them, but which they see perfectly clearly from the very beginning.

There's a change of government in Uruguay, and the incoming authorities, finding themselves in need of money, reappraise local tax rates throughout the country and then launch a ruthless attack on holiday resorts, where they know there's a glut of easy and, moreover, foreign money. Municipal taxes suddenly skyrocket. Water, which had previously been practically free, is now pure gold. The weather rebels. There's a series of inclement, treacherous summers, with furious downpours of rain that always catch them out just as they arrive at the beach, forcing them to change their plans and turn around, and then clear to reveal flawless, sunny skies just as they pull the car up to the garage back at the house, resigned to waiting it out. They'd console themselves with the pool, now that the problem of its inexplicable structural incline has been resolved (*rugby guy!*) and it's possible to fill it properly with water—except that the brand-new owner of the adjoining property's ruthless tree-felling (which they were the first to celebrate, thinking they'd get a much better view without having to spend a single penny) has made it unusable, like a runway, a tunnel for an anarchic wind that constantly threatens to break into a storm.

They begin to go less often, and for fewer weeks at a time. The Beast grows resentful. A particularly rainy winter (along with a not-entirely-legal new construction growing a little higher up the slope, held up by rickety scaffolding) unleashes an avalanche of mud, rubble, and a few unsuspecting construction workers, burying part of the right wing of the house and exposing a certain inherent weakness in the foundations (*rugby guy!*), which let in much more humidity than they should, resulting in an unavoidable process of excavation and resealing that lays claim to tons of money (though money is *always* measured in tons when something needs to be fixed), as well as a summer and a half (measured by the Uruguayan clock) of use of the house. They start to lose their tempers. They're burgled (while one of the sitters is in the house: they lock her in the laundry room, and the children, who are in the garden tempting guinea pigs out of their burrows with insecticide tablets, don't even realize what's happening). They hear a rumor that someone's planning to build a B and B for backpackers on the spot that's home to a grove of magnolias they love. It gets harder to find friends to go with them. The windows cloud over with salt residue: all they can see at breakfast is a sad, lumpy white veil, with the sea and the coast and the little terra-cotta tiled roofs behind it in a blur, like an old postcard of a forgotten place. The house is huge, pointless, impossible to heat. Drafts whip through every door and window. When a shutter (one of the beautiful Mediterranean shutters the rugby guy campaigned for so ardently) comes loose and begins to flap, they can spend up to twenty minutes trying to track it down, frozen stiff. Sometimes—usually at night, when they're beset by the terrible insomnia that strikes during vacations and they each withdraw to contend with it alone, ashamed, like injured animals—they feel as lost and alone there as intruders.

When they're on the brink of going bust (if only they had a company that could go bust, or anything more tangible than the chaos of blind transactions, financial juggling acts, hopeless business prospects, and ever-more-meager accounts that now constitutes their respective inheritances) and sick of their money disappearing into the Beast, which swallows it as regularly as Sonia receives her remittances from the beyond, they decide that it's time for the house to give some money back. They don't have any grand ambitions. They're not hoping to get rich. They just want it to pay for itself. Someone—probably a prompt hired by the former rugby coach—suggests that they convert it into a time-share complex. When they call him to discuss, the former rugby coach turned architect and now apparently mind reader, since he seems to have known all about it before he's even picked up the phone, unfolds the plans (which he mysteriously has with him) and, in a tone of boundless enthusiasm, details a plan for remodeling. That's what he says: *remodeling*. He's planned for every eventuality; the most important thing to him is to put their minds at rest from the start. Since it's so spacious and generously proportioned—it's almost as though he foresaw this the first time he drew it!—nothing needs to be added to the house, not a single brick—except, of course, what's required by the current regulations on time-share apartments: communal spaces; three, or maybe two, yes, just two more tiny little bathrooms; the extra sixteen square meters they'll need to add to the pool; and parking spaces—crucial: who would stay all the way up there without a car?—for half a dozen vehicles. They'll work with what they have. Divide up what's already there. They could get half a dozen apartments out of it, and the seventh, a duplex, the best and most expensive apartment in the development, would be theirs for three weeks of the year, whichever they liked, and they wouldn't have to pay a penny. Construction can start today, now, yesterday even, if necessary. The ex-rugby guy happens to have some people in the area ready to work—a Filipino-style bungalow complex that had to be abandoned because of a little financing hiccup. It'd be as simple as sending them to the Beast instead. When could they get the advance together so work can start?

The project is a failure. They plan to open in December, in time for high season, with a view to quickly earning back the cost of the work. But a nasty winter, legal setbacks that are slow to work themselves out (rugby guy's contact at town hall having been arrested for the little matter of corrupting minors), and rugby guy's disappearance for a month and a half—which he says he spends in a foul-smelling hospital in Maldonado being treated for a string of lung collapses, but which according to the house sitters, who bump into him twice at the currency exchange in town, he spends holed up in the casino, wearing flip-flops, tinted glasses, and a floral shirt bearing the bungalow complex's logo; wherever he is, it's a long way from the construction work, which grinds to a halt, inspiring a furious union protest, complete with two days of peaceful occupation of the Beast and the smell of chorizo sausages in the complex's future lobby—all combine to delay the cutting of the ribbon until the chilly month of May, when only an outlaw on the run would rejoice at the prospect of a stay in a time-share on the Uruguayan coast, and thus begins the saddest case of lost profits in the history of summer architecture.

This phase lasts ten years—more or less the same amount of time it takes Sonia to go from adoration to weariness, until one day she turns him out onto the street with a cardboard box full of clothes (minus the items she's bought him during their time together, all of which are in exquisite good taste, particularly that tweed jacket, and which now fit the delinquent like a glove) as well as a plastic bag containing his dream diary, his little medal, his envelope full of baby pictures, his die, and his tin frog, which is still leaping around in thin air, like a badly castrated cat investing the remaining drops of its instinct in copulating with stuffed toys like an absentminded robot; and a piece of paper torn untidily from the phone pad that lists the days and times of his visits with the delinquent, who for good or ill has ended up growing fond of him. In ten years, the Beast passes through more than one change of identity; every time, the house sitters act as figureheads (the only demand his mother and her husband successfully uphold throughout the whole process), and every time, it's all in vain. There's a first attempt at time-sharing, which starts off well (with 80 percent occupation) but soon dies out, having been eclipsed by the mania for all-inclusive resorts and their exclusive hedonism. After that come three years as an eco lodge; years of ugly forest-green paint and solar panels that can never make up their minds to work. Then another bid at time-sharing, a concept that's won back some followers during an interim of economic crisis, recession, and unemployment. From then on, it's free fall. It becomes the headquarters of a burgeoning local property development firm that goes under the same year it moves into the Beast, whose owners, a pair of incestuous cousins, have to be forcibly evicted by the police, leaving behind them a year's unpaid rent, utilities, and local taxes. It's the part-time headquarters (for long weekends only, since they're perfect for marathon sessions of psychodrama, sensory perception, transcendental meditation, and yoga) of a fraudulent "holistic health clinic" that contacts them via the rugby guy, who has recently been named consul or military attaché or first secretary of the Argentine embassy to South Africa, where his old friends on the All Blacks await him eagerly. It becomes a production house and, later, a film studio, first for ad spots (the pool in that soda ad, the spiral staircase where the husband gives his wife two tickets to Punta Cana, the big living room with the chimney and the built-in bookshelves where those twin brothers wage their chocolate-cookie war), then for two or three experimental films that are never screened, in which the production house's director ends up investing (and losing) the little money he's earned, and which, according to the few surviving members of the cast who are prepared to talk about it, turn into huge, pointless orgies (the guy has high blood pressure and diabetes and is incurably impotent). At the end of this tunnel, the Beast is a wasteland, a Xanadu with no electricity and almost no glass in the windows, where the wind plays outlandish harmonies and animals sleep and reproduce; which even the house sitters have fled (after auctioning off the little remaining furniture, their only means of getting their outstanding pay), and which isn't even entirely theirs. Hoping that it'll bring in an injection of capital, they signed 40 percent of the partnership over to two associates—another architect and the owner of a tourism company—who are even less sharp than they are.

"That's it. It's *over*," his mother tells him one afternoon, with her coat still on and her shaking hands twisting her purse out of shape while she sits on the edge of a two-seater wicker chair that, even though it's impertinently ugly, is the only thing that could be called furniture in the studio-pigsty he moves into after Sonia throws him out: "We've split up. I'm living in a hotel. And I'm out of cash." Standing up, he can only manage to ask: *What does that mean.* He's wearing the orange terry-cloth robe that sometime later he will take to the hospital his father's staying in, having grown tired of seeing him patrol the corridors in his old jogging pants. It's the only thing he can think to say. He skims over the news about the separation. He's thought about it so many times that it's as though it had already happened. He's not even interested in his mother. It's that phrase that interests him. What does *I'm out of cash* mean? The phrase alone, in and of itself, beyond the expression of awestruck stupor on the mouth that says it, and beyond the low, subdued tone of voice it's said in, the tone of someone speaking through sleep or medication. He knew it; he's always known it. But now it's his mother who knows it, while he—beaming and looking as simple and radiant as the picture of an idiot—is in disbelief. It's like something we've witnessed a thousand times in films or in our dreams or in other people's life stories suddenly happening in real life; something that can't surprise us because we already know every detail. It doesn't surprise us: it freezes our blood. Not the event itself, but rather the supernatural, absolutely miraculous dimensional shift that must have taken place in order for it to break through the shell surrounding the world it normally occurs in and travel to ours and turn it on its head. "'What does it mean?'" his mother repeats, now looking at him for the first time, with a mixture of disdain and compassion. And the answer: "Nothing. It doesn't mean anything."

Ah, if only he could have given the same response every time he's been asked the same question. Why hasn't he ever been able to? Why has he always preferred to have something to say rather than nothing? Who made him the guardian of the supposed meanings of things? There's his disabled group, for a start, whose members are always so desperate to know everything. For a few months, no doubt to fool himself that he's not a kept man, he agrees to watch and discuss films with a group of culturally curious sexagenarians, a sort of private film society. They meet once a week, always at a different member's house. They don't pay much, but the payment is rhythmical, regular—the closest he's come to a job in many years. The disabled bunch—as he calls them, inspired by the leader of the gang, a brilliant, extroverted retired accountant confined to a wheelchair by a degenerative disease—are kind and welcoming. The women crown every meeting with a big ethnic feast (hummus, falafel, goulash with spätzle), offer to fix the button dangling from his jacket, and show him their family photo albums, casually pointing out the niece or granddaughter who might suit him. The men offer him cigars and slap him confidentially on the knee before asking him who he's planning to vote for—almost all of them started out on the left, and though they no longer belong to that past, it still dictates their gestures, behavior, reactions, and manner of speaking, like a country they once fled and have no intention of going back to, though they owe it everything and will never forget it—or offer him their varied contact lists in case he needs a loan, a discounted refrigerator, or free printing for some wedding invitations. They all trust him, invest him with an authority he doesn't have, and swallow in wordless, reverential silence the sprawling Soviet and Czech and Hungarian films he shows them in order to ingratiate himself to—or maybe finish off forever—their legendary militant youths.

Very soon, though, their reserve dissolves and they grow more confident, and when they come across a dense, studied image on the screen that they don't understand but can tell is full of meaning, fit to burst with it, they finally pluck up their courage, raise a shaking hand, and ask: "What does that mean?" That's how it begins: the disaster, the epidemic, the domino effect. What does that mean, that sled that's lashed by snow in the glass globe that falls out of the dead man's hand? And what does that mean, that old workboot with no laces that's been left in that ruined anti-aircraft shelter? What about the darning the heroine devotes herself to in the final scene, when she's surrounded by toothless, homeless wasters? And the old spinning top that never stops turning? And the two song verses the protagonist tries in vain to remember, which come back to him only at the end of the film? And that broken window, that stained petal, the clock that tells the time backward in that old bar in a Portuguese port?

He answers, of course. He answers like the good slave he is to the only real job he's ever had, a job nobody offered or assigned to him, which nobody hired him for and in which he never has to answer to anyone, a job he's born with and will die with: taking responsibility for the meaning of things. But he can't stand these people. He'd desert them, leave, slamming the door behind him so that it shook and possibly cracked the beautiful crystalware the disabled bunch keep unused in heavy, dark-wood dressers that are always threatening to collapse, which they somehow managed to bring from Europe in one piece, the same wild Europe that slaughters all of their relatives, or fills them with lead, or gases them—he'd desert them if he weren't suddenly distracted by the new member of the group, a tall, thin man with an aquiline profile who's as stern as an undertaker and has a vague record of militancy (he's rumored to have provided printing machinery to the Montoneros), who spent six years in exile in Brazil, where he first heard and uttered the word *reciclaje*, selling out, and then came back and made a fortune, initially importing blank videotapes, then later manufacturing them in a remote Patagonian plant, until he retired and used his remaining stock of tapes to start a small distributor of art-house films called La Tierra Tiembla, whose titles—Soviet avant-garde, Italian neorealism, German expressionism, Jancsó, Wajda, *Jackal of Nahueltoro*—are listed in alphabetical order in a brochure the accountant slips into his pocket one night, all of them at his disposal for the group's meetings, all he has to do is ask. The other members of the disabled bunch call him the King, an innocuous abbreviation of the King of Magnetic Tape (but the King, being modest and antimonarchical, must never find out). Whatever his powers might be, the King doesn't contain the epidemic; quite the opposite, in fact. The what-does-it-means gain force. Maybe the element of novelty he adds to the group makes the desire to participate and to know even stronger; maybe the fact that the films they're now watching and discussing come from within the group gives them more of a right to make themselves heard. Chaplin: what does it mean. *Ashes and Diamonds*: what does it mean. *Stalker*: what the hell does it mean! One more and he'll explode. He really will leave this time. He'll take the money for the last session and never see them again. But now it's *Ivan the Terrible*—one of La Tierra Tiembla's star titles, along with *La tierra tiembla*—and if he left before that, as he intends to, he'd miss the best thing of all. He'd miss the King of Magnetic Tape's lesson.

A rainy Friday. A spacious, comfortable apartment in a prosperous, though not opulent, neighborhood. Waterproof jackets and umbrellas dripping penitently in a half bathroom. Steam rises from cups of coffee and tea and smoke from the King's Cuban cigar while he gazes at the screen wearing a broad smile of satisfaction, just like he does every time they watch a film from his list. As teacher, he stands guard near the machine, his leg trembling with impatience. He has the remote control in his hand, his finger ready to fire as soon as one of the usual hunters of meaning—the chocolatier's pallid sister; the man who owns a printing company and never stops rubbing his nose; even the accountant, so emboldened by his colleagues that for some time now he's been launching his what-does-it-means along with grand, accusatory gestures, as though the wheelchair were a pulpit and he a latter-day tribune—raises a hand and spits out the stupid question that he will once more, perhaps for the last time, to his shame, do everything he can to answ—but sshhh!: they've just crowned the young, embattled tsar. The crown has already closed around his head, he's already been given the scepter (or rather has grabbed it from the archbishop himself with a hand that's covered in rings, in a decidedly inelegant show of greed) as well as the globe with the cross on it, and the hairy old maniac is already singing his hymn in a voice that comes from beyond the grave, and now two members of the court enter the scene and take up position on either side of Ivan, two steps up, and a pair of servants gives them two large bowls, which they hold by their shoulders. The chorus erupts. The courtiers tip the bowls, and a rain of gold coins falls on the tsar's head, it falls, and falls, and won't stop falling, a long cascade of gold that skims the crown and his shoulders and spills onto the floor, and when it seems as though the gold will never stop raining down, the chocolatier's sister lifts her soft buttocks very slightly from her mustard-colored corduroy chair, points at the television, and says, "What does it mean?" Having seen it coming, he presses PAUSE immediately, without even turning to face the television again (he knows the film by heart), and solemnly, or wearily, stands up to speak (it's the last time, he thinks, the last!), and when he opens his eyes after emerging from the brief blackout he dips into in search of literature on coronation rituals, he sees eight faces contorted by stupor, eight stunned masks, plus one—the King's—that's frozen in an expression of horror, and which then suddenly turns red and breaks into a coughing fit. Out of pure momentum, he starts to speak: "Well, on days of celebration in the tsars' Russia, gold was . . ." The disabled bunch's faces all remain exactly the same. Nobody's listening to him, nobody even registers his existence, bewitched as they are by the monstrosity before them. At this point he turns around and sees on the screen a washed-out close-up with the enlarged grain of an amateur recording, in which two colossal cocks, as knotted as tree trunks, are charging simultaneously on a woman lying facedown. He's not sure whether he lets go of it or it slips out of his fingers, but the remote control falls facedown on the floor, also stunned, and the tape starts rolling again. A change of scene. Shot from a meter, maybe a meter and a half away, the picture is crystal clear, as clear as the cascade of gold that pours down on the young tsar of all Russia or the Portuguese shouts of ecstasy that spark into the living room like obscene fireflies: a dark-skinned stud, standing up with his legs slightly bent, fills her ass, while the other one, a white guy, lies beneath her, ramming against her cunt and squeezing the flesh on her buttocks with his long masturbator's fingers. Five seconds later, the Brazilian trio return whence they came, like a monster being swallowed by the lips of the cave that spat it out, and the golden coins start their interminable falling again.

How she—her, his mother—would love for that to happen now, with all her helpless heart: for money to rain down on her. She says it just like that, with her eyes lost in the ceiling moldings as though waiting for the first notes to drop from the little crevice someone's crudely restored with plaster, where a spider is sleeping at the bottom of its web, curled up into a ball, while the smell of its prey slips into its dreams. It takes him a while to figure out how little this desire has to do with ambition, or with the sort of lovingly cultivated toxic rancor a queen would accumulate over the course of decades of exile spent putting on a public display of indifference to news from home, and then by night clipping and saving that same news in the always slightly damp, or suffocating, or noisy privacy of her rented room. Actually, his first thought when she confesses her bankruptcy is that what she's really confessing to is a crime, a crime of lèse-majesté like child abuse or massacring a people, and that the victim of that crime is him, her son, who's been dispossessed of everything that's rightly his by the simple act of confession. He might owe her his life, as they say. But she owes him money. A lot of money. For an exhausting fraction of a second full of early mornings, aspiring lawyers loaded down with files, echoing hallways, and coffee from machines, he imagines himself taking his mother on, bringing her to justice; he even hears himself delivering his dispossessed son's plea before the judge, who's suddenly downgraded—because true justice is impervious to the imagination—to a narrow-shouldered secretary with dandruff who stops typing to ask him, "*Excess* has an *x* and a *c*, doesn't it?" But who would he call as his witnesses? His grandfather. His grandfather, repatriated for the solemn

duration of the hearing by means of spiritualist subterfuge . . .
His grandfather, of whom sometime later, when there's still
less left of the nothing she confesses to having that afternoon,
his mother will tell the story with a face that's red with fury,
as though it had happened moments ago and not fifty years
in the past, of the time she came home from school and, still
excited after the indoctrination she had received in the subject
that morning—"Saving is the foundation of fortune"—asked
him for a savings book, and he, giving her a little push as
though she were blocking his line of vision, told her that he
had "a bank account, not little savings books."

No, it's not ambition; it's an absolute lack of hope, a sudden, frozen emptiness that opens in her chest when it becomes clear that she doesn't have a peso left. This is what
condemns his mother to wait for the demented miracle of
money raining down from the sky. Less out of conviction
than because they're within her grasp and as fresh as ulcers,
she starts with reasonable miracles, clinging desperately to
the idea that sooner or later the Beast will be sold, no matter
what state it's in, no matter what time and the winters and the
humidity and weeds and gangs of squatters with backpacks
have done to it, and that she'll recover at least some of what
she lost. She hasn't been back for a long time; she hasn't witnessed half the metamorphoses it's gone through; she can't
even picture it any longer. Every image she has of it is out of
date. She remembers it only in dreams, on the rare occasions
that she manages to sleep uninterruptedly, and the payback
for those interludes stolen from insomnia—a miracle that's
almost more unheard-of than money raining down: she has
her own table set aside in the hotel bar, and the night guard
knows to switch on a light and serve her some tea or a glass of
cognac when she comes downstairs with eyes like saucers at
three or four in the morning—is a vision played at high speed
of a type of creeping citadel growing constantly and in every

direction, including down into the earth, following a system of interlocking cubes through which all manner of frightened little creatures pass in and out: moles, armadillos, guinea pigs from some useless experiment, which a psychotic stylist has decided to dress up in tiny rugby shirts. "It must be worth something," she thinks. And if there's no value in the house, in the grounds, the cement, the floor tiles, the window frames, the flagstones, or the mosaic tiling, then there must at least be some—just like in tales of adventure in which, for all his charisma and virtue, the hero always owes much of his appeal to his nemesis's monstrosity—in the tragic role the Beast has played in her life; in the way in which the house lays waste to everything in the space of ten years.

Sitting in the hotel's picture window in her nightgown, with her beautiful Italian raincoat hanging from her shoulders, getting a little tipsy from the cognac fumes, she daydreams about someone who hunts for grisly scenes in real estate, one of the vultures that patrol the stars' neighborhoods in Hollywood with checkbook and pen at the ready, searching for ruined or abandoned mansions with blood spattered on the marble in the bathroom, the gold ceilings embroidered with bullet holes, poolhouses decorated with brain matter. Why not. Why shouldn't she be blessed by one of these evaluators of misfortune. It must be worth something. But if anyone were to ask her what "something" means, how she measures "something," she wouldn't know what to say. *Nobody* would know what to say—just as committees of experts brought together to value the masterworks of idiotic artists, or idiotic works by masterful artists, don't know what to say and can never reach an agreement. When she comes back down to earth and reassesses, and decides that only modesty will save her, she imagines small amounts, just a bonus, the difference that would understatedly but decisively remove her from this nightmare from which she can't seem to wake up. But she waits, and she waits, and that modest little amount that would make her happy never comes, and once again the Beast becomes everything to her, responsible for taking everything she had and capable of giving it all back, and at those moments she opens her hotel room's window in the middle of the night, in her nightgown, with her Italian raincoat falling off her shoulders and onto the floor, still completely unwrinkled, no creases at all except the ones the designers intended to be there, and she yells at the world, at the sleeping world of Calle Uriburu, the astronomical figure for which she's prepared to talk—only to talk, she won't guarantee anything beyond that—about selling the house. It's clear, in any case, that the one possibility his mother never considers, neither in her moments of modesty, when she just wants to forget, nor when she's overcome by the desire for revenge and she screams for the whole world to be signed over to her, is the ridiculous, paltry, disproportionately sad figure they end up getting from a Uruguayan construction firm, the last on a long list of buyers—and the only one that agrees to actually *see* the house—who disappear one after another when they see the photos: ten thousand dollars, to be halved with her ex-husband.

She's almost in tears when she shows him her five thousand—a stack of fifty-dollar bills in a dirty, bulging envelope with a lottery ticket stuck to it like a stowaway, peeping out surreptitiously until she hides it in irritable embarrassment by shoving it to the bottom of her purse—under the fluorescent lights of the bar she arranges to meet him in after collecting it, a strange place—all tinted windows, with waitresses serving in their underwear and all wearing the same dark wig, like replicas of an original from Le Crazy Horse—two blocks from the basement office of the construction firm's Buenos Aires sister company, or maybe it's just the den of its team of accountants and lawyers. She raises the hand holding the envelope to call the nearest stripper—yes, it's a dive, but the cheesecake is unbeatable—and he catches a neighboring regular following the gesture with a look of murderous longing. "Let them rob me," she says disingenuously, and then, still crying, she blithely waves the bills in the air in a bid to divert the stripper's attention away from a client who's asking for clarification about the menu while staring at her chest. "What's five thousand dollars compared with everything I've lost?"

This wasn't exactly what she had in mind when she imagined money raining down. As a result, she doesn't use it to alleviate or anticipate necessities, but rather as a sort of restorative compensation, damages for the misunderstanding of which she's once again been the victim. She packs her little suitcase, settles her bill at the hotel, and waits until nighttime to say goodbye to the guard. And then she moves and spends all of it, down to the last fifty-dollar bill, at a slightly better hotel (three and a half stars, although the half star on the neon sign doesn't always light up) on Calle Juncal, two blocks from the last one, with an elevator, cable TV, and a basket of umbrellas in the lobby for rainy days. She had envisaged something more unexpected and drastic, the type of downpour that's unleashed without warning and changes everything, for good or ill, like a doctor holding an X-ray to the light, clearing his throat, and pointing at a laughable little white cloud growing hesitantly in the middle of the pancreas. She was thinking of a true event, the type that always intrudes in such an untimely fashion in old romance novels, with a visit—announced by a bell that shreds the tranquility of a home that's had little to do with the outside world—or a letter in a tattered, worn-out envelope, its address so poorly written that it's been lost and sent back and forth several times before arriving at its destination, and even run the risk of not arriving at all.

For example: Ángela. At the age of twelve, she befriends

a sullen, skinny girl with very bony knees who spends recess clinging to the railings in the yard, trying to hide the monstrous platform shoe that completes her right leg. She frequently lends her her protractor and ruler, shares her lunches with her, lets her copy her tests. One day while either winning or losing at hopscotch or elastics (it's just as boring either way), she abandons the game and makes her way to the railings at the other end of the yard with her head held low, and then, somewhat warily, enters her ostracized orbit. She stays there with her for the rest of recess, leaning on the railings and gossiping rapidly about each and every one of the classmates she likes or pretends to like during the day, like a spy hurrying to transmit the information she's harvested, until after a brief spell of surprise and shyness Ángela joins in and starts doling out her own lashes in a delayed frenzy: the stitching coming undone on Berio's shoes, Melnik's bad breath, Venanzi's zits, Serrano's fake tits. They spend months this way. On the last day of school, while they're leaving class in a flock, as they always do, Ángela takes advantage of the general confusion to put a piece of folded paper in her hand and asks her not to read it until after she's left, and then, as they reach the door and her driver gets out of the car and starts to head toward her, kisses her very quickly, grazing the corner of her mouth with her lips. She never sees her again. Her family moves and she changes schools, or maybe they move overseas. But fifty years later, when she's more of a millionaire, more crippled, and more lonely than ever, who else would Ángela write to again but her, his mother, asking to meet up; who else would she tell that she's sick and putting her affairs in order, and that after considering and rejecting a relatively scant list of obvious candidates, she has decided to leave her entire fortune to her.

That's the kind of rain she's hoping for. But will it ever come, if she hopes for it so desperately? Will it ever come, if it's less rain than late payments, the type of delayed satisfaction that no creditor ever truly forgets, even if only because they've made a note of it somewhere in their little book of debtors? Conquering her reserve about telling people of her change of lifestyle, she circulates the address and telephone number of the hotel she's living in. Among the calls she receives, which she gaily filters through the hotel's reception, there's only one she doesn't recognize. She repeats the name aloud and searches for it fruitlessly in her address book. She asks a couple of the old friends who over time have become emergency memory sources. Nobody remembers it. It's unknown, faceless, untraceable, and impossible to pin down. "This is it," she thinks. This is the secret: that there are no clouds or thunderclaps; that the rain truly comes from the beyond. She gathers her courage (a siesta, a shower, two glasses of cognac, three lines of written prompts on how to sound surprised, what tone of voice she should use, and how thankful she should be) and makes the call. It's answered by a nasal voice that thins every now and then into a dramatic and artificial-sounding falsetto. He blurts out her married name—the excitement of getting a callback, no doubt—and then tries to cover the slip by coughing until he realizes that he doesn't know her maiden name. He's a former stockbroker. He used to manage—quite solvently—some shares his mother bought on her ex-husband's advice (and then sold at a loss between the Ecolodge Period and Time-share Mark II, in order to replace all the flooring in the Beast). He's set up on his own now, still in finance. He's offering some very advantageous opportunities, and going through his portfolio of good former clients ... Might they meet up for a coffee? He got her new number from her ex-husband. Incidentally: What's all this about living in a hotel?

Though she dreams of a downpour of money, he's the one who ends up getting wet. His father dies. One night he waits for the nurses to make their last rounds, unplugs his tubes and wires (the morbid pleasure of the tape crackling as it comes away), and crosses over to the room opposite in his bare feet and orange robe, where a former Boca Juniors midfielder hooked up to a dialysis machine is waiting to play poker with him. The night nurse—the tall, severe one who doesn't accept tips—finds him in a chair next to the midfielder's bed, very rigid, with three sevens in one hand, his head leaning slightly to the left in an attitude of elegant mistrust, and the other hand resting on the edge of a table on wheels that's serving as a makeshift baize, where the deck (with the seven of clubs on top) and a plastic cup containing two fingers of whiskey sit waiting for him.

The coffin shrinks him and makes him look ugly. A very long white hair comes out of his mustache, does a double somersault, and embeds itself in the side of his upper lip, very close to the corner of his mouth. Has his beard been trimmed? He argues with someone who works at the funeral parlor about the shroud they've put on him, which is made of white linen and very similar to the one they used at the hospital because they didn't have anything else, only more sheer, almost transparent, a ridiculous, feminine little piece of baby's clothing that looks as though it belongs on an angel. "Why don't you give him a harp, too?" he says, and leaves, slamming the door behind him. At one point, when he's left alone with the body, he leans over his face, takes another close look at the wrinkles on his forehead that he knows so well, and kisses him. The temperature of the body makes him recoil. It's a cavernous cold, like marble, dense and abysmal; a cold that will never change, that will stay this way forever. His mother, who to his surprise is the first to arrive and the only guest who takes the starting time to heart, stands up throughout the whole service, keeping her vigil with her umbrella and purse in hand. Out of loyalty to the old law of punctuality and stoicism as means of sharing in others' pain, she refuses a seat and rejects water, coffee, and the repulsive mints that a gaunt raven in a suit brings around every now and then on a plate, with his other arm folded gently against his back like a waiter at a pretentious restaurant.

There aren't many people at the wake; most of their faces are hazy, and though they signal to him determinedly from someplace in the past, he doesn't recognize them. *Acquaintances.* His father spent his life surrounded by transitory, furtive people, whose ties to him were always circumstantial or contingent. He tries to remember who they remind him of while he accepts their hugs, pats on the back, and distressed or encouraging words. He recognizes a couple of employees from the agency; the now decidedly obese money changer who used to change his dollars while the house was being renovated; the doorman from a building in Belgrano where he'd get trapped in the elevator on two out of every three visits; the blond, slightly wall-eyed woman from Air France or Alitalia, who would always point at him when he accompanied his father on his payment rounds as a boy and ask if he could make one like that for her. When the time comes, though, it's not these guests but rather five doleful strangers—one of whom has a deep tan and tries to stifle an attack of allergies by pressing a handkerchief to his nose—who help him to carry the coffin, while the undertakers' cars double park and everyone disperses into clusters of dark sadness, some following the procession to the cemetery, others leaving. His mother leaves. She gives him one last hug, jabbing him slightly between the shoulder blades with the handle of her umbrella, and he suddenly breaks down in tears like a little boy; he breaks just like a little boy when he cries. In the arms of that shrunken body, which he would never have believed could contain him, he's struck for the first time by the certainty that he is the only tie there ever was between his mother and his father. She dries the tears from his face with a finger, tells him that the cremation would be too much for her, and asks him for twenty pesos for a taxi.

Doors slam shut, engines start up, a gear stick groans, there's a monosyllabic froth of goodbyes. Normality—a red light, a cleaning-supply store open for business, a woman sweeping her balcony with a shawl on her head—pierces him like a scandal. Someone removes the white letters spelling out his father's name on a sign made of black cloth and replaces them with different ones. G-R-O-L-M-A-N, they say. He could swear it should be a double *n*. Mr.? Mrs.? He'll have to come back at three, when the Grolman service starts, to check. He looks for something or someone to tell him what to do, what to say, where to go: a sign, an instruction manual, one of those promotions girls in tight skirts and too much makeup who can show you how to get a loan or configure the latest phones in the space of two minutes. How can "how to behave at your parents' funerals" possibly not be a compulsory class at school? An open door appears in front of him, and without thinking about it he ducks into a car that smells of leather, leather so fragrant it seems fake. They wait for a few minutes. There's a trio of ravens deliberating next to the car in front, the one carrying the coffin. The driver of his car has protruding ears, very short hair, and a string of tiny warts across the back of his neck. He distracts himself by looking at the tinted city, now as dull and dark and muffled as on a cloudy winter's evening. His eyelids are heavy and his body feels numb, like it's been padded with layers of damp wool. He's suddenly grazed by a very old memory of his father: he's fallen asleep watching TV with his mouth wide open and is snoring at a cartoonishly high volume, as though there's some kind of broken machine stuffed up his nose. He'd so like to fall asleep. In fact, he is beginning to sleep, to dream— a point-of-view shot of his hand grabbing a handle, a door leading to a garden carpeted with water, the cawing of a sort of paper toucan that flaps its wings as it passes—when the door opens and into the seat beside him, as delicately as if he were invisible or a part of his dream, slips the stranger who sneezed while carrying the coffin.

In less than a minute—the time it takes the driver to pull away, maneuver around the car in front, and turn onto the road under the hostile gaze of the ravens from the funeral parlor—they've cleared up the confusion about the cars. No, the car isn't part of the procession: it was just parked where it shouldn't have been. It's the cab the stranger picked up at Ezeiza Airport, which he just flew into from Brazil, heading straight to his father's funeral and now to the cemetery. No, there's no need to get out. On the contrary: it's an honor for the stranger to share this journey with him (sneeze), sad as it is. He smiles at the stranger dopily. They're driving down a boulevard lined with auto-parts stores. The driver steers almost without touching the wheel, giving it the merest grazes with his fingertips, like a gloved magician or someone who specializes in treating infectious diseases, and seems to shift gears with nothing but a gesture, not making any contact with the stick. "This is Avenida Warnes, isn't it?" says the stranger, admiring the display cases full of tires, the Formula One streamers in the windows, the signs tattooed with the names of car manufacturers, and the blow-up dolls waving to attract clients. He hasn't come to Buenos Aires for twenty-two years, and (sigh) he wasn't able to meet up with his father that time either. He offers him a soft, sweaty hand that's wearing a wristband made of small, multicolored beads. "Beimar," he says. "Milo Beimar."

"Beimar ... Beimar ... ," his mother repeats, as though turning over a suspicious mouthful. The name means nothing to her. She can picture him at the funeral: his elegant, well-cut, expensive suit and his mafioso's black shirt and tie, and

that carrot-orange tan that looks like it came out of a bottle of
Sapolán Ferrini. But his face is like a white wall. She remembers wondering who he was, but she wondered that about
90 percent of the faces she came across at the funeral. She
didn't recognize anyone, and that didn't surprise her. It was
like that even when she was married to his father. A new face
every day, people appearing and then disappearing without
a trace, voices calling, asking for him, and then hanging up,
never to call again. She never even has time to register their
names, so she can't ask him about them. What happened to
Barbat? And Desrets? Don't you see Desrets anymore? They're
like imaginary friends. At a certain point she starts to think
they're all extras, bit players that his father, who's always
been so sensitive to what other people think, hires to simulate
a social life, a network varied enough to create the impression
that he's a man of the world—an impression he can't live
without—in just the same way that his monogrammed shirts
and cufflinks claim a lineage he doesn't have.

He likes this idea of his mother's. It's tortuous and precise, with just the amount of spite any idea needs in order
to go out into the world and hit its mark. But bit player or
otherwise, Beimar was and is somebody. For a start, he was
the Man Who Owed His Father Money—and the moment he
says it, he sees the title printed on a cheap horror-film poster,
in big red letters that flicker like flames—or (a subtle change
in viewpoint, or genre, to children's horror) the Man His Father Goes to See Every Night in Rio de Janeiro, Leaving Him
Waiting Up Alone at Hotel Gloria. To sum up the fragmented
service record that Sapolán itemizes through his sneezes between Avenida Juan B. Justo and a cemetery on the outskirts
of the city in Ingeniero Maschwitz, which has no tombs or
headstones and looks like a golf course, a pristine carpet of
grass so green and smooth that there's no earth on Earth capable of growing it: Milo Beimar, a precocious, provocative

underground filmmaker, expelled for reasons of sexual rivalry—half an hour of wild sugar harvesting in the former cane capital, Tucumán province—from the tiny, secret group that captured this landscape for the first scenes of the revolutionary documentary *The Hour of the Furnaces*, and from Argentina on political-criminal grounds; the bearer, on boarding at Ezeiza Airport, of a flawless fake passport, a one-way ticket to Rio de Janeiro, and a suspicious handful of genuine dollars (all three things the fruits of his father's machinations); an exile in Brazil, where he becomes a convert to the cinema of the advertising industry, drowning in money and drugs, the new drugs of the late seventies; a wreck, in the eighties, from the money and drugs of the seventies, which cost him a septum, a marriage, and all of the assets, minus what goes to his wife, acquired during ten years' work in the advertising department at the Globo network. That's where he is—with no job, no money, and no family, living on handouts in the maid's quarters of the spectacular Ipanema apartment of the junior writer at the agency whose scripts he spent a decade filming—when his luck changes. One night after leaving a friend's house (one of the few he has left besides the junior writer), completely deranged after hours spent watching TV, drinking bad beer, and smoking good Brazilian marijuana, he walks aimlessly for a few blocks (it's a cool night, there's a pleasant breeze blowing from the lagoon and drying his sweat, and passing from east to west in the moonless, starless sky is a Boeing 747 that will plunge headfirst into the Atlantic in the early hours of the next day), and is suddenly struck by the blood-sugar dip he was expecting later, when he was already safe and sound in his little cave at the junior writer's place, within easy reach of the demented quantities of ice cream his host keeps in the freezer for just such occasions. His mouth is very dry, and the edges of his lips sting. In a sudden moment of synesthetic self-awareness, he sees them shining in the darkness, outlined by four very fine lines of yellow lightbulbs, which flicker like a landing strip in the middle of the night and then go out one by one, as though his lips were about to fade away. He's dying for something sweet, and there's no store in sight. The only thing he has on him is two sticks of the sugar-free mint gum that several pseudo-dentists with bright eyes and very taut skin have recently started to promote on TV using whiteboards, pointers, and misleading arguments written by the junior writer who's taken him in and his underlings at the agency. Better than nothing. He puts both sticks in his mouth at once. A minute later—by which time they've lost all trace of their flavor—he has no craving for sweets whatsoever. His blood-sugar levels have completely stabilized. He goes to sleep. The following morning, he wakes up early, showers, and uses a public phone box—since there's nobody less trustworthy than the junior writer—to call the lawyer who handled his divorce, to whom he owes two or three times what he owes his father, and fill him in on his nocturnal discovery. Two months later, the two of them seal an unofficial deal, in absolute secrecy, with the company that produces the sugar-free mint gum: the company transfers several million to his almost empty checking account (a sum he's lived on ever since, is now living on, and will probably continue to live on without needing to work until he dies), and, for his part, he promises to withdraw the lawsuit claiming large-scale fraud and endangering the public health that his lawyer wrote in a morning and half of an afternoon.

And now the brilliant illumination of that toxic, hopeless night seems suddenly to be delivering a check—like a holy apparition breaking through a canopy of black clouds—which Beimar fills out with his crude handwriting, signs, rips out with a sharp, expert pull, and then hands to him in the cab on the way back from the cremation. It finished less than half an hour ago, and already he can barely remember it, as though the flames that charred his father's body had also swallowed all trace of the ceremony. He'd go so far as to swear that it didn't happen at all, that it was just a figment of his imagination, if it weren't for the urn sitting next to him on the backseat of the car and the prayer card he's holding between his thumb and index finger. How did it get there? One of the ravens must have given them out to the mourners at the end of the ceremony. He hasn't taken his eyes off it since they left; he's in awe of the artistic technique—it's a retouched photo of his father, tinted with pale colors like something from a comic book or a picture from a children's story—which softens his features and gives him the smiling bonhomie of a saint. Until he has to switch hands to take the check that Beimar hopes will settle this debt he's had for, what, forty years now?

Someone once told him—perhaps to ease his mind, perhaps because they were sick of hearing him complain about his family's erratic financial management—that you don't inherit debts. The phrase has an immediately soothing effect on him. It has the impersonal air of incontestable law, at once understated and apodictic. He later confides it to a friend, with a relief as eager as if he were sharing news of a recently discovered cure that will save his life, and the friend tells him that no, indeed, you don't inherit them—as long as the dead person doesn't leave anything to pay them with when they die. It's an unexpected nuance, but it doesn't worry him. He knows that other than the dry lemon; the withered lettuce; two old suitcases full to bursting of photos, postcards, and letters; the tweed jackets in the wardrobe; and his jazz records, his father has left nothing. But with the check in his grasp, he feels a certain alarm. Now there *is* something. What if the creditors who haven't lifted a finger so far because, like him, they assumed that there was nothing, suddenly show up en masse, like armies of hungry ants? He's comforted by the fact that there's no evidence of the check's existence, or of the debts';

there are no receipts, no documents, nothing, no witnesses, no testimony. It's just one more of the informal transactions carried out in furtive tête-à-têtes, between individuals and outside of any legal framework, following unwritten rules, rules that might never even have been established—arrangements that are more like secret trysts than financial deals and which little by little, on a macroscopic scale, are beginning to occupy more space and gain a footing, and which end up prevailing as an alternative order, a corrupt order that's as contagious as a plague-infested body but also as vital and powerful as the legal body it was born to compete with.

But for some reason, though he's ecstatic to find that's he's rich, and through the best possible means, the only means he and his mother find irresistible, incomparable—rich by the work and good grace of the dead—he doesn't cash the check straight away. He puts it off time after time, justifying this behavior to himself with all manner of flimsy excuses. He's scared, that's all it is. Even without imagining the creditors' eyes flashing as they lie in wait in the bushes, he always ends up nervously replacing the check in the bottom of the drawer he put it in on his return from the cemetery. Looking at the bottom of the drawer is enough. The check is proof, testimony, documentation. On his way to the bank the day he makes up his mind, he stops and thinks: What if it's fake? What if it bounces? What if as soon as she reads the account holder's name or types in the number, the cashier frowns and stops smiling, asks him to wait a moment ("the system's crashed"), and uses the finger she's been skinning with her teeth since she was thirteen years old to push the red button hidden beneath her desk, thus alerting the half dozen undercover Interpol agents guarding the bank?

But nothing happens. Or it does, though not the thing he fears most, the thing that terror has turned into a foregone conclusion in his mind—the only place, incidentally, where he trusts that things happen—but something else instead; it's not necessarily better than what he feared, but it's different and thus unrecognizable, a mirage and a nightmare at the same time, and for a few days he sinks into an amorphous shock, a kind of imbecility, living an unreal life, a life that's not his own and that he wouldn't be able to describe, as though the deeds that have been done, far from returning him to reality, have imprisoned him in the abstract wasteland through which he's now wandering, which is neither imagination nor reality but what's left—desolate and bright and utterly unnuanced—after the kingdom of the former has been lost and the latter is the land of dullness par excellence, and thus intolerable.

He doesn't even think about the basics: the calculation Beimar must have carried out in order to arrive at the figure he writes without a moment's hesitation on the top right corner of the check, as though he's had it in his head for a long time, since long before a mutual friend called to tell him about the death of his father, whom he hadn't seen in more than thirty years, and he decided to take the first plane to Buenos Aires in order to get to the funeral on time. "You've been conned, for sure," his mother tells him when he admits that he took the check without asking any questions. He omits to tell her the amount, out of prudence, but as soon as he decides to keep it to himself, the word itself flashes in his head momentarily—*amount*—seeming pregnant with strange possibilities and more valuable than any sum of money it could possibly designate. He doesn't tell her how much, just that it's enough, and she doesn't ask any questions. But it's precisely the modesty of the word *enough*, its reasonableness, that makes her suspicious. No one suddenly repays a thirty-year-old debt that nobody has claimed with a sum that's just "enough." And anyone who pays such a debt so reasonably is without doubt paying less than he owes; much less than he'd

owe if the accounts were done properly, including the interest, late fees, and fines necessary to bring such a long-unpaid
debt up to date. He gives her some credit—because the fantastical amount awakens equally fantastical speculations in
him—but otherwise takes it for what it is: the knee-jerk reaction of someone for whom money is, by definition, something
of which there's never enough, which is even more true with
money that comes from men, that despicable breed of de-
serters, cowards, and loners, and above all else of incurable
misers. She's a sensitive judge of large and small amounts,
and she's good—very good, as though the skill or common
sense she lacks in practical financial matters flourished in ap-
plication to idle, utterly inconsequential musing—at working
out whether the amount charged for some good or product is
sensible or inadmissibly excessive. But don't come to her saying that a sum of money is "enough." Not to her, please. By
the way, she needs a little cash to collect her reading glasses:
a broken arm, a new prescription, something of that sort that
she announces hurriedly and doesn't bother to explain, as
though to explain would be to humiliate herself and under-
mine the entitled tone in which she always addresses him. He
hesitates for a second. Without looking at him, she does what
she does every time she asks: allows herself to be absorbed for
a few seconds by the very slightly loose clasp on her purse,
some stitches coming undone on her sleeve, a new freckle
on the back of her hand, any one of the banal surprises she
seeks refuge in whenever she's taken a risk, as earnestly as a
child who believes she can make herself invisible by closing
her eyes. "How much do you need?" he asks, looking for the
first age spot on the back of his own hand. "Two hundred and
fifty. Two seventy would be better, so I can take a taxi straight
there. The optician closes in fifteen minutes."

No, he doesn't ask himself how Beimar arrived at the
figure, nor does he make any of his own calculations, nor

even ask his mother to help him out with any. He gives her the money for the glasses—end of story—and then stops a taxi for her and watches her get into it slowly, seeming a little bewildered, with the irritated or affronted air that tends to come over her whenever she has to negotiate worldly things, like taxi doors, for example, and her purse, the height of her seat, the hem of her raincoat, the distance to the door handle she has to pull closed once she's sat down; things that weren't made with her in mind, as she realizes for the nth time with a despondent sigh before distilling her indignation into her tone and giving the taxi driver the address like an impatient boss: not her when she was young and beautiful and queenly and didn't need them (but when, dear God, when was that?), nor her now that she's no longer queen and she needs them more than ever. Rather than crunching numbers he'd get lost in halfway through, before he's gotten anywhere, disoriented by the multitude of things he doesn't know, he prefers to be lost from the start, deliberately, thinking of the winding, treacherous path the money took before coming to him, a little, he thinks, like an astronomer—as though the world of astronomy were more familiar to him than financial calcula-tions—working out how many light-years a star must have traveled before becoming what it is now, a mere spark on the black cloth of the sky. It doesn't matter what his father did for him—and Beimar doesn't say a word on this subject, only repeating the phrase *what your father did for me* like a litany—or what it cost at the time; he thinks of it as a meteor traversing history at varying speeds, sometimes breakneck and unstoppable, other times with difficulty, crawling along and battling fierce resistance like a kind of intrepid hero on horseback—like the protagonist of a novel he reads with great interest when he's young and feels the saddest disappoint-ment on finishing, but which doesn't really have an effect on him until many years later, when he's stopped thinking about it, at which point it makes such a strong impression that he decides he's never read nor ever will read a better book in his life—a meteor that passes unceasingly through superhuman epochs, tearing through them like a wild beast tearing through paper rings at the circus, and changing all the time—personality, class, and especially gender, but never age—and which at a not-particularly-memorable bend in this tortuous road comes across a fearful blond boy who, though he never sees it, can't stop thinking about it, about the shapeless phantom it is to him, while he tries to get to sleep in the hotel room in which he's been left all on his own. How contemptible, how unpleasantly obtuse the dollar seems, the so-called *green* or simply *bill* (as though it alone had the right to be made of paper), being always so cautious and always exactly the same, in comparison with this champion of metamorphosis on whose skin history never stops stamping its mark: pesos moneda nacional, pesos ley 18.188, pesos argentinos, australs, simply pesos ... One of today's pesos, he thinks, for example just one of the three hundred he gives his mother that afternoon—figuring that, since she finds it embarrassing to ask, if she asks for two hundred and seventy she must really need at least three hundred—would be worth ten billion of the who-knows-how-many pesos moneda nacional his father paid for the fake passport, the ticket to Rio de Janeiro, and the wad of real American dollars that saved Beimar's skin and helped him to start a new life. But astonishing as it is, this equivalence is also neutral, it doesn't mean anything, in fact it disregards and tries to erase from memory the prodigious catalog of adventures that made it possible, the dead ends, forests, and abysses it's founded on, the danger and madness that have fueled it.

And so when he goes to his father's apartment, it's not really to clean, as he tells the doorman when he bumps into him in the lobby, nor to get his father's few possessions in order, as he tells his mother, nor to fill the two industrial-size trash bags he takes with him with all the things that need to be thrown out, but rather to find proof that the debt existed. The apartment is filthy. He can tell it is as soon as he gets inside and starts groping his way through the darkness, feeling a little uneasy—he's only now realizing how foreign this space is to him, how infrequently he came here to visit his father—and smelling the rancid perfume of confinement and damp wood—ah, his father's passion for wood, which was almost as fervent as his feelings about paper—as well as a harsh odor like old wool that gets inside his nose and tickles it. He lifts the blind halfway, until something blocks it and the cord suddenly stops dead in his hands: yellowish walls, a whole baseboard of accumulated grime, the floors stained and carpeted with dust. A cockroach scurries away, its body slightly tilted. He crushes it under his foot and a galaxy of corpuscles shatters in the air and dances in the ray of sunlight shining through the window. His father is dead and the sun is shining through the window.

He opens the fridge, finds the half lemon and the limp lettuce sitting alone on the cracked glass shelf, as orphaned as he is, and looking at him with an air of irritation that suggests he's just interrupted an intimate scene, and closes it without touching them. He will never touch them, not even when the time comes to get rid of the fridge, when a neighbor buys it for spare change, along with some old speakers, an adjustable nightstand, a weighing scale, a Continental typewriter, and an unused nutcracker with the price sticker still on it—a lot the neighbor puts together himself after inspecting the apartment in a professional sort of way and carries away on his back as casually as if it were a bag of feathers. If he could put a date on this filth, he thinks, he could also date the moment his father started to die. It's not when he's taken into hospital; not the diagnoses or the operations or the secret diet of whiskey and pretzels he shares with his poker rival at the hospital on a few of his nights there. It happens while he's still in his apartment, in possession of all his faculties, and surrounded by the minimal cast of objects now surrounding him—things he didn't even want or choose, things that had belonged to his mother, for example, which he never had the courage to throw out and so dragged from one year and one apartment to the next, and which survived it all and ended up prevailing over him—the moment he looks around with his hands on his hips and decides he won't clean, that it's not worth it. And falls into his TV chair. That's when his father starts to die.

Everything is dirty but in its place. Dust and order are only incongruous in living things. They always come hand in hand in those approaching death. Records in alphabetical order by artist, the same as the books. The first hangers for coats, the next for jackets, the last for pants, never mind that every garment has the coarse texture of objects that nobody has touched for years—a covering of filth that sticks to the fingertips like wax. He finds his notebooks on the coffee table, at an angle to the corner. There's a trail of semicircles and parentheses printed on the wood leading up to them, marks left by wet glasses and cups, the universal symbols of neglect. He opens the first one excitedly, hoping to find his father's handwriting, the strange mixture of upper and lower cases with random serifs that look like loose threads, always leaning to the right and growing gradually smaller, as though something were crushing his hand as it moved—handwriting that he's never liked but which he nevertheless copied for a long time, even though his teachers and his girlfriends, who were apparently incapable of deciphering his essays or making out the names and numbers on the notepads next to the phone, reproached him for it on countless occasions.

He finds figures. Or rather they leap into view, insects hungry for a three-dimensional life they might have been dreaming of for years. Series, strings, whole columns of numbers that start on the first line, aligned to the left, and carry on line after line to the bottom of the page, then go up and start at the top again, like echoes of the column just completed, then carry on again to the bottom of the page and start again on the first line, to the right of the column they've just finished, and so on for pages and pages. Every now and then there's a variation that turns the page into a kind of extraordinary oasis, a vision of graphic freshness: shorter columns, with accompanying words that allow him to decipher them—words like "travel costs" and "extras," like "income" and "expenditure," words like "Enrique," "electricity," "tips." From time to time there's a loose sheet slotted in, a letter on letterhead, folded diary pages, Post-its, bar napkins, flyers from the street, discoveries that gleam with promise for a moment, and which he pounces on excitedly before putting them back again, sadly, as soon as he realizes that they haven't escaped the awful reach of these accounts: expenses from a weekend in Tigre written on the back of a flyer from a riverside grill, an inventory of outstanding payments on an envelope from a large hotel, a list of commissions earned over the course of a month on the rectangular card of a bookmark. From the first page to the last, from the first notebook to the last—there are seven, all the same brand and bought in the same place, an old bookshop near the courthouses—the figures grow smaller and more pinched, filling the empty passages that had made it possible to distinguish them, determined to colonize every last bit of space with their swarming. Finally, in the last notebook, the only spiral-bound one, the columns twist and brush against one another, the numbers are illegible, the pages skies full of backlit locusts.

Sitting there on the arm of the TV chair, leaning over those seven open notebooks, he cries all the tears he didn't cry at the hospital, or at the funeral, or on the afternoon almost a week later when he suddenly gives a worried start in his kitchen while making coffee, as though remembering something important that slipped his mind too long ago, and thinks, "I have to call my father!"—and in that same moment the evidence that he's dead forces itself upon him. The apartment is so quiet that he can hear every tear hitting the paper. The numbers shatter and blur into blackish, reddish, violet-tinted streaks that tremble and ripple gently for as long as it takes the paper to absorb them, and are then still. He remembers a scene from a film about the life of Chopin: the gradual, delicate dripping of real pulmonary blood that splatters the keys while he passionately attacks them. For a moment he marvels once more at his father's pride and belligerent boastfulness in proclaiming that he's never had a bank account and never used checks, that he flat-out rejects every credit card offer he receives, even the most advantageous ones—the worst of all, he says, faithful as ever to the principle that evil is never as ruthless as when it wears a benevolent face. He doesn't want to be controlled by money. He doesn't want to see his life reduced every month to a summary drawn up by some poor bank worker with a dirty collar and pants coming undone at the cuffs, one of the walking corpses dragging their feet that his father teaches him to recognize on the street while he's still a boy and urges him to avoid. He doesn't want other people to know who he is because they know what he buys, what he spends his money on, how much he pays for the things he wants; much less does he want them to tell him what they know. But all things considered, those seven notebooks are precisely the thing he detests, only written by his own hand: his autobiography in accounts. In a certain sense, this is his life's work: the only testimony he sees fit to leave of himself, the document that shows where he invested his resolve, his faith, his scrupulousness, his concentration—all the valuable powers he would so often lament not having.

With a little attention and an ounce of common sense, anyone looking at these books could reconstruct everything his father is and does during the last years of his life, all the things that nobody who was there with him could ever reconstruct from what they saw or witnessed by his side. Anyone—but not him; he knows he won't even take the time to clear a path through this jungle and track down the only thing he cares about: how much Beimar originally owed. And that same afternoon, after trying on two tweed jackets, attempting to wash away the layer of mildew and rust in the toilet with a long stream of piss, and definitively breaking the blind, he drops the notebooks in the bottom of a trash bag. It's not the striving for an impossible cleanliness—the cleanliness of dying without a single peso but with the books balanced—that makes him cry. It's not the candor with which his father ends up denying himself the very freedom he accuses the world of trying to take from him. He cries because he's just caught him in private, in this fragile, obscene intimacy, and seen him doing uninhibitedly, with no concern for modesty, exactly as he really wants to, the only thing he does because he can't help it, because he would die if he didn't. He cries because he's never seen him this way before, naked, surrendered to his cause, the cause of numbers; and he cries for the absurd, solemn fervor of it, and for the stubborn, comfortless solitude to which it always condemned him.

And then his mother succumbs to a delirium of requests. She doesn't just need help buying herself a heater or a new coat at the beginning of winter any longer, or having new carpet put in the little apartment she moves into, or finally replacing the contraption on which she struggles to complete her translations, a slow, purring machine that frequently quakes with distant digestive crunching, which she inherited from the stereotypical rich friend who suffers an attack of generosity three times a year, for no other reason than that she wants a change of scenery, and begins to give things away left and right, using members of her court to liberate herself of all the trash cluttering her palace: furniture, lamps, works of art, clothes, electrical appliances she has no idea how to use and has never even taken out of their boxes.

Sometimes late at night—very late, at the hour when the only things that happen unexpectedly are mistakes and tragedies—the phone starts to howl, and he answers it still half asleep, thinking that if he can find his glasses on the nightstand, where he thinks he left them, and put them on, even if they're upside down, he'll be able to hear better, to understand what he hears better, or pretend to for this interlocutor who can't see him, and then his mother's voice spills a few drops of desperate lucidity into the labyrinth of his ear. She doesn't shout, she's not forceful, everything she says is very measured, but her voice comes to him from another hemisphere, a strange, polar world, or the desert, somewhere where it's always daytime and everybody's always awake. It's two o'clock. While going through a pile of bills she thought she'd already paid, she's come across a warning from the electric company: they're threatening to cut her off if she doesn't pay her balance tomorrow. At three thirty, the vacuum's swallowed an electrical adapter, or a keychain, or a ball of yarn, and is now snoring and coughing and blowing instead of sucking. Where will she find the money to get it fixed, since she hadn't planned for this? At six, she's just discovered, to her horror, a warning of extra costs in fine print on her monthly maintenance breakdown from her building's management.

It's the wonderful world of contingency, simultaneously varied and monotonous, that bursts in with each of these nocturnal cries for help. His mother, the only undeniably necessary presence in his life, a fundamental, originating, indisputable element, is now a realm of accident and uncertainty that ruins every plan. Sometimes, when he's resigned himself to suffering these early-morning attacks, he thinks that perhaps he'd like them more if they took a different form. He misses—as though he's ever actually experienced these things—a certain turmoil, the drama of hearing someone shout and their voice break, the operatic kind of desperation that can shift huge bodies of air around immense spaces with its pompous gestures, all key elements of an emotional realism that he doesn't necessarily believe in—he is his mother's son, after all—but which he wants to think would compensate, at least in strictly theatrical terms, for his being washed up onto the brittle shore of wakefulness once he hangs up the phone, after promising to get the money to her first thing in the morning. But his mother hates, has always hated, theater's bombast, its eruptions, its sentimentalism, its sense of exaggeration. She asks, and she really is desperate, but the rhetorical model for her desperation isn't a scene of catastrophe—which though they're striking and sultry are also vulgar and always a bit humiliating—but rather rocky insomnia, which has everything she needs in order to be as dignified as a deposed queen: calm, dryness, tension, and the impression—which only seasoned connoisseurs can really appreciate—that everything is fine, in its place, in order, where it should be—apart from *one* thing, just one, something that's not at all obvious—an eyelid that's been fluttering for hours, her trembling hands, the blinding clarity of small or distant objects—but that will end up blowing everything to pieces.

One day it's a root canal, the next the annual fee on her credit card, the next she's a little overdrawn on her savings account. By the time he chooses to notice what's going on, he's become a crucial figure, a lifesaver, a financial ambulance who shows up, or should show up, with fresh money in his pocket as soon as he receives the alert. He's become a drug to his mother. Sometimes he travels halfway across the city to pay for a cheap breakfast that's been holding her up in a shabby bar, and the face she greets him with when he gets there sends a shiver down his spine. She's always at the worst table in the place, the one closest to the restroom, in a draft, or threatened by the corner of a murderous window, looking very serious and concentrating very hard on something that only she can see or hear or feel, and she always has her coat on and her hands clamped around her bag, as though she thinks she's about to be robbed. She says horrible things about the waiters, complains about the volume of the TV, and pushes her half-eaten meal away with a gesture of disgust, while a terrible volatility brews around her mouth, disrupting the thread of grooves that has accumulated above her upper lip over the years.

She never calls to ask him to pay. She wants the money herself. She wants the exact amount she needs, no matter whether she's paying for a carrot-and-lettuce salad, a consultation with an osteopath, or an overdue bill for some plumbing work that takes her bathroom out of service for a week. He arrives, his mother tells him how much she needs—they're always very precise amounts, often including centavos—and once she's got her hands on the money, she suddenly gets impatient, keeping her mouth shut or giving him short, reluctant answers; treating him distantly and with disdain, like an acquaintance who's taken too many liberties with her, and with the resentment and the same combination of pride and spite with which addicts spurn their dealers as soon as the fix they would have done anything for just ten minutes earlier is safely in their pockets.

Why doesn't he just give her what she might be asking for: a reserve? There's no great mystery in living hand to mouth, on the bare minimum. It's an art that doesn't require juggling skills, as is often supposed, but rather modest virtues: sobriety, a little order, a certain degree of calculation. But for someone who's used to relying on what's known as support, someone who has always enjoyed the indulgent protection of means, savings, and investments; who has permitted herself the luxury of not knowing what they are, where they are, how much they're worth, or how they grow, but not the peace of mind they confer, not the levity with which they would allow her to face the future, feeling as radiant and optimistic as a traveler arriving in a foreign city very early in the morning, after an exhausting journey, and washing and going straight out, without sleeping, to lose herself on unknown streets—for someone like this, who's been blessed for years by the existence of such a secret supply, it could be the most terrible of all nightmares. She who has lost everything has lost much more than her fortune. She has lost the precious margin of time her fortune granted to her, the interval, the magic buffer that shielded her from the immediate experience of things. Losing everything condemns her to a hell worse than poverty: the hell of living in the present.

He simply doesn't trust his mother. If he were to give her the famous reserve, he thinks, not reproachfully, in fact forgiving her because the logic is so familiar to him, she would be incapable of saving it, she'd spend it all immediately, in a kind of trance, out of fear of dying and leaving behind, untouched, some capital that could have made her happy, or in the grip of the frenzied desire for revenge that's always waiting, in varying degrees of hibernation, in every ruined woman. She'd soon be just as desperate as before: drowning in the hardships of daily life, eaten away at by fear of her most dreaded specter—the unexpected expense—and then devoured by the guilt of having spent the money that would have allowed her to confront it.

She admits as much herself when she tells him that in her dreams about having money—which she has more and more frequently, and not only at night, while she sleeps in the spartan setting she's chosen for herself in an attempt to, as she says, take the bull of money by its horns, but also during the narcoleptic episodes she succumbs to at all hours of the day, on the bus or in the rheumatologist's waiting room, sometimes even while she's translating, in between two intractable paragraphs—there's only one thing that can definitively ruin the dream, much more effectively, even, than knowing that she's sleeping (another frequent occurrence): the certainty that any amount of money would be too little, far too little for her aspirations, too little to fill the hole that need has opened in her chest over the years. *My thirst for revenge has grown too strong.* A reserve would be an option if it were possible to turn back the clock and start again from zero. But his mother doesn't have zero in her. There's always some prior balance that grows a little every day, silently and ceaselessly and out of all proportion—minus five, minus twenty, minus a thousand—which any reserve would have to redress. But what kind of perverse reserve would deny the future—by definition the only thing it should be concerned with—because it's obliged to settle the debt of the past?

She dreams about money, often about just seeing or touching it. When she returns from these dreams, she always feels a vague ache, as though she's been grazed by the wing of one of the lascivious monsters that poke their snouts between curtains and prowl around sleeping women in paintings. Even when she's engrossed in her work, totally absorbed by whatever she's doing, deep in the state of repetitive anesthesia to which her daily life has long been reduced, it only takes one unexpected sign—the shriek of the buzzer or the phone, both of which, to her bullheaded pride, ring ever less frequently within the four walls of her house, and even then generally only to announce an irritation like the knife sharpener, a traveling salesman, a couple of preachers, or a telemarketer—to jolt her from her stupor, startle her awake, and have her standing in front of her bedroom mirror, quickly preening herself and putting on something different, a silk scarf or the only hoop earrings she hasn't sold, the enormous black glasses that make her look like a grasshopper, anything that will create the right impression for the lawyer or notary she supposes has come to see the mysterious beneficiary of the concession, the donation, the legacy that some dead man or woman has entrusted them in their dying wish to pass on.

As soon as she finds out that someone from the past is looking for her, she forces her memory into action; she spends a whole afternoon cleaning the cobwebs from that storehouse full of useless junk and doesn't give up until she recognizes the person's name, can picture their face, and finally, lost in the folds of a school-day morning, a birthday, or a scene from a childhood vacation, finds the secret favor, the mark of complicity, the support she once offered disinterestedly, simply out of friendship, for which the recipient of her generosity has now come to repay her, sixty years later. Peeping into her own childhood, her youth, she notices that everything is slightly different: there's the same theater of torment, the same darkness, the same damp cold that soaks her to the bone, but while she drags her feet like an anguished soul, without anybody seeing, sometimes without even being aware of it herself, her little frozen hands drop a few seeds like secret messages to posterity.

Suddenly, a small court of new friends springs up around her. They circle her with a languid intensity, like the old moths they are, and die out quickly, in the time it takes for her crazy hopes of inheriting something from them to vanish. She introduces him to one old misanthrope who's as shrunken as a raisin and very elegantly dressed, with whom she says she shares a Sunday-morning ritual of reading the papers in a bar. That and Verdi's *Luisa Miller* are the only things they have in common. He is irascible, vain, rude. He's never bought her a coffee. He won't give up a single supplement—not even the women's one—until he's finished reading the whole paper. But he's all alone, and very sick, he probably won't make it through the winter, and it would be unforgivable to let his box at Teatro Colón, his car and driver, and his weekend place in Colonia be orphaned. When he asks her what it is that she likes about these circumstantial relationships (he knows her, and he's grown tired of seeing her ill-temperedly reject every stranger that approaches her), she cites either intimate reasons—she likes to be able to *talk* to a man, for example—or bluntly selfish ones: she wants to take this trip; she needs the air, the thermal baths, the quiet. She won't be able to finish the translation that's been giving her so much trouble anywhere but at this Trappist retreat in Córdoba, but when she gets back after a two-week vow of silence and military discipline, dying of hunger and not a single line further in her work, she soon sets about flaying the depressive lesbian she really went to accompany, who drove her crazy talking about her millions and her travels, but realized when she went to pay for their stays at the monastery, as promised, that she had forgotten her wallet. She's always the one who finds a new bar, stops saying hello to them, and loses their phone numbers, once she's sick of everything she has to put up with in order to spend time around them, and disgusted with herself, with the absurdity of her own aspirations. She emerges feeling sad and gloomy, as though hungover, but she chronicles her misadventures with a humor, an attention to detail, and a cruelty he would never have imagined in her.

More than once she calls for help and asks him to meet her in the middle of one of her broke girls' get-togethers, as she calls the gatherings full of nostalgia, cake, gin, and free-flowing gossip that she enjoys with half a dozen fellow travelers at an old-fashioned café in the basement of the oldest, most antiquated mall in the city, whose perfunctory music—bossa nova, Henry Mancini—she professes to love, along with the brothel-worthy insouciance with which the waiters' jackets and pants—modeled on bellboys from old hotels, in red with black buttons and black with vertical red stripes down the sides—accentuate the muscles in their backs and buttocks. More often than not, he shows up to find them talking about money, in sentences that, more often than not, start, "When I had money ..." The rest of the time, for variety's sake, it's "When you had money ..." His mother always sits in the same spot, facing the door that leads to the street. This way she can see him arrive and get up in time to cut him off before he comes too close, and the rescue can be executed out of sight of the other women (who, of course, start discussing it immediately).

As time passes, she grows impatient, as though something were beginning to drain away from her. It's a tyrannical impatience that predates her requests, making them angry and as abrupt as orders. It's no longer enough for him to say that he'll get the money to her. She feels as though she's being treated like a child, like rather than helping her he's simply trying to distract her and soothe her anxiety, as though needing money were nothing but the façade of some greater problem that's at once deeper and more vague and can be relieved only with kind words rather than money. She wants to know when, where, how. Any distance between the request and its satisfaction is too great. Things could get in the way, anything could happen. He could have an accident, she could have a heart attack, the economy could collapse, the peso crash, all in the space of one night, and the cash would never reach her. She needs it now, immediately. And anyway, she won't be able to sleep, and then she'll feel groggy and won't be able to work (she translates on average three thousand words a day, which means that losing a day of work means losing three hundred pesos) or even get dressed, and she'll end up going back to bed, exhausted, not to sleep, because she knows there's nothing more elusive than lost sleep, but to lie there on her back with her eyes wide open, asking herself the same question she always asks: How long will she wait this time before taking the pills that will knock her out?

Irritation notwithstanding, the urgency poses less of a problem when the bouts of need strike at reasonable hours. They agree on a time and a place, which enables him to reorganize his activities around the rescue mission, and he observes them scrupulously, out of pragmatism more than any sense of responsibility, like doctors who are punctual only in order to save themselves their patients' reproaches. She thanks him—in her own way, of course, avoiding any explicit display, or rather drowning it in a show of compassion, saying how sorry she is for the inconvenience the emergency must have caused, the commitments he must have had to postpone, et cetera. But very soon, something about the meticulousness with which he carries out these missions—a bureaucratic zeal that's as efficient and reliable as it is impersonal, being apparently immune to specific circumstance—starts to enrage her, and suddenly becomes the target of her spite. She treats him as she would an irreproachable but insipid employee, giving him double-edged praise and exalting his virtues while making sure he's aware of the enormous area of requirements he does not satisfy. Seeing him arrive fresh from the shower very early one morning, dressed with the middling elegance that's perfect for a long day filled with a variety of demands, it occurs to her to suggest, half laughingly, that she pay him: not for the money he gives her (about whose return she never says a single word, though they're always "loans") but for bringing it to her. It would be simple: he could just keep a small percentage of each sum he brings. But soon the nocturnal calls intensify, and at ten past three in the morning, when his arms are dead and his eyes full of sleep, and the city is frozen,

the good offices of the exemplary messenger aren't so appeal-
ing, and the smile with which he receives and disarms her
sarcasm during the day becomes a weary grimace. Nevertheless, he agrees once, having been alarmed by the crisis pitch
of her voice and the racket drowning it out—the telephone
receiver being dropped, some glass smashing, Verdi playing
at crazily fluctuating volumes—and then a second time, and
while he makes his midnight journey like a dealer of cash,
something dawns on him with absolute certainty, simultaneously scandalizing him and filling him with awe: there aren't
any other sons crossing the city at this hour to take money to
their mothers. He promises himself he won't do it again, and
the decision alone is a relief. But he knows how much he'll
miss the bright light that floods his mother's face when she
gets out of the elevator on each of those insane early mornings and comes toward him to open the door, holding herself
very upright and smiling, as if she'd regained the only thing
whose loss she'd ever truly cried for—much more, even, than
her fortune: the radiant beauty of youth.

He offers to send the money by cab from then on. "That's
all I need!" she shouts from the other end of the phone: "Here
I am, terrified that the cash will never get here, and you want
to give it to a bunch of thieves." He persuades her: there's a
cab company he trusts, he knows several of the drivers, he's
used them to send things before and never had any problems.
The system seems to work. It's simple, efficient, and, insofar
as it's based on money—the charge account he opens with the
cab company—unequivocally professional, a trait for which
his mother has always had a particular weakness, partly because it makes the tortuous misunderstandings that come
hand in hand with personal relationships impossible. She
likes professionals. She trusts their uniforms, their overalls,
and their diplomas, and above all the fact that their expertise
can be accessed only with money. She's always won over by

loquacious doctors with gray sideburns who write with gold pens, shuffle technical terms like cards, and can check her lymph nodes with their eyes closed, but she doesn't throw herself at their feet until she receives the signed, sealed bill for their services; when the diagnosis, treatment, and soft parting pat on the shoulder have been reduced to a number, no matter how inflated it is—the higher the better.

Some nights she calls him, asks for the money, and then lowers her voice a little, her timidity just barely shot through with lust, to ask if it would be too much trouble to request the driver who came last time, Walter, Wilson, Wilmar, in any case a Uruguayan with prominent cheekbones and an enormous nose, a relic from the fifties who wears V-necked sweaters, checked shirts buttoned all the way to the top, and freshly shined shoes, who always declines her tips with a vague air of surprise, looking like the last bastion of civilization declining a barbarous old custom, while tilting his head to one side and brushing the brim of his hat with two fingers. A week later, the whole system is endangered. At quarter to four, his mother calls him sounding raw. Where is the driver? He should have been at her house an hour ago. Why didn't he send him? But he has a crystal-clear memory of ordering the cab. He calls the firm, and a cavernous, cigarette-sanded voice tells him that the delivery—a sealed envelope with the recipient's name clearly handwritten on it—was handed over at two forty-five on the dot at the agreed address. Incidentally, says the voice, after a long, deep hack that seems to produce a couple of centuries' worth of mucous sediment, is sir a close relative of the lady who received it? In that case, could he explain to her that the company's drivers—least of all Wilson, who doesn't drink and is married with two splendid daughters—are not allowed to drink alcohol with clients in hallways at two forty-five in the morning? He calls his mother. "The money never came," she says, blowing her nose. "You can think what you like: it's their word against mine." She's indignant but also shivering from the cold, and from total exposure, as though she were calling from a barren land swept clear by a freezing wind.

This scenario is repeated twice. Both times—partly because he can't bear to hear his mother whimpering down the phone, and partly because every discussion with the man with the cavernous voice ends the same way, abruptly, with a hail of coughs that nearly makes him pass out—he ends up getting out of bed and going to her place to give her the money, the second version of the money he's already given her. On both arrivals he's surprised by the metamorphosis that's taken place in her: she's glowing, calm, looking as though she's just stepped out of some sort of miraculous floral bath, and dressed as if she's going out, and she asks if he'd like to have breakfast with her. But there's a third time, identical to the earlier ones in every detail, and this time he decides it's gone too far. After enduring a sprinkling of exclamations from his mother ("I told you, darling! They're crooks!"), he puts on his coat and goes to the cab firm's office in a fury, and right before he pushes the door open, he recognizes Wilson-Wilmar-Walter—his hat poking out, narrow turnups on his suit pants, his dress shoes' leather gleaming like porcelain—polishing his cab's steering wheel with an orange flannel while the radio spits out a song that's as gooey as pomade: "*Pretty little baby / Vidalitá / Sad baby girl / How little is left / Vidalitá / Of what you once were.*" He stops dead. How long has it been since he last shouted at someone? How long since he was so close to another human face? The last things he remembers from the skirmish are an extreme close-up of the button on Walter's checked shirt hanging loosely from a thread that won't last long, the soft echo of an old-fashioned cologne, and a small, probably malignant mole in the shape of a club stuck to his prominent nose like a sticker. But what right does he have to stockpile these shreds of reality while the one who's fainting and bringing his orange flannel to his chest as though in adoration and staring at him with confusion in his eyes while his knees give out is delicate Wilmar, poor Walter, incorruptible Wilson, all three of them innocent, all three victims who as he's been told a thousand times will take any journey, no matter how dangerous, be it to Barracas, Fuerte Apache, or Lugano, but not to that frazzled diva who comes downstairs with a bottle of Grand Marnier and two glasses to accept the envelopes her son sends her.

The last he hears of his mother—news she tells him herself, when she calls to ask for cash for her taxi, and which he files away next to the image of the button on the checked shirt, the cologne, and the mole (false alarm: it was benign)—is that she goes to visit him in the hospital—angina: nothing his Uruguayan even temper can't negotiate without struggle or complaint, and with a casual, flea-market kind of grace—and that there, under the hospital's high surveillance, the patient of the three Ws ends up accepting the clandestine drink he's always rejected on his mother's doorstep. After that, there's no news for a while. He realizes this one afternoon when he's at home alone and the silence seems to solidify around him. He sees then that those imperious requests, those early-morning phone calls that so exasperated him but that he ended up putting up with, were the only contact he had had with his mother for a long time. And now that he hasn't received one for days, a strange terror floods him. He's scared to call her. Scared that he'll call her and she won't answer; scared of going to her apartment, ringing the buzzer, and getting no response; scared of convincing the super to open the door and finding her in bed with the remote control in her hand, or stretched out on the black tiles in the bathroom, struck down while plugging in the hairdryer. In truth, he's scared that finding her like this might be his mother's last wish for him. It's not exactly a suicide scene that he's imagining: given her sense of the ridiculous, she could never have done something so deliberate, so solemn and laborious, without laughing and ruining it halfway through. No: what he fears is a chance, accidental death that has nevertheless been imagined so many times that the spectacle of its consummation couldn't, now, exist without him, its recipient and the only reason she's imagined it so many times. And, of course, he wonders how she's getting by without asking him for cash. He begins to run through all the possibilities that occur to him, rapidly, like a slide show—his mother as a beggar, his mother as a thief, his mother filling out a translation with long, pointless periphrases to increase the number of words she'll be paid for—but they're immediately eclipsed by another thought: what *he* will do with the money he doesn't give to her. What will he use that trickle of bills for now? Not that it even amounts to much. It was a drain, yes, but more because it was so relentless, so rhythmical, than because of the quantities involved. And yet even so, that modest but unforeseen surplus makes him feel affluent and magnanimous, fills him with new energy and an obvious, textbook philanthropic urge, the type that's born of money itself rather than any particular sensibility, will, or ethic—of money and the special logic it obeys of its own accord once it reaches certain thresholds of abundance, which he so reviles in rock stars, successful artists, heads of technology corporations, and other contemporary magnates. Yes, he could be a benefactor. Why not? He could inject some cash into a factory and turn its structure upside down. And then money would finally replace revolution.

But where to start? If only they were still producing that beautiful Trotskyist monthly, all black type on red pages, that his friend's older brother lobbies him to contribute to as a teenager, which he supports however he can, siphoning small donations from a monthly allowance that's already too small to satisfy his basic needs, namely fast food, the cinema, and his first black-tobacco cigarettes. Of course, back then it's not the money that makes him do it: neither what it means for the Trotskyist monthly's finances (which are pinned together so precariously that much like his mother—the mother who's disappeared and is showing no sign of life—they can't allow themselves any luxuries, certainly not that of any extra costs, and much less that of reducing the contributions of sympathizers like him, no matter how insignificant they are), nor what it means to have money, given that to be precise he has none at all. No, he does it out of terror. (He understands this now, forty years later, once his mother has stepped aside and disappeared from view, emptying a vital space in which long-dormant forces can now wake up and congregate and do battle again, as if his mother's suffering were ultimately nothing but the latest incarnation of what other people call or called *the people*.) Not terror in the sense of the intimidation (always tinged with a certain excitement) worked on him by his friend's brother and his fellow militants, who are always full of talk of the working class, the bourgeoisie, the party, imperialism, the general strike, permanent revolution—words that he always hears in capitals and visualizes as charging colossuses, a gang of monumental monsters that can circumnavigate the planet in three paces and that reduce the world of girlfriends, football, records, and hanging out in plazas he shares with his friend to a sad, pygmy dimension; he sees the group in action together only once, at a meeting his friend manages to smuggle him into, which, like most Trotskyist gatherings, is spent in interminable smoking of cigarettes, drinking of coffee and maté, and, in the small hours, gin, and above all in "defining the situation," an art in which there never has been nor will be anything to rival Trotskyism. No, it's terror in the sense of terror: terror that he'll be identified, kidnapped, hooded, tortured; terror that he'll die like a dog, be thrown in the river or blown up, for having donated those centavos to a monthly publication that even he, though he supports it passionately and endorses everything it says, from the first word to the last, or maybe for precisely that reason, closes thirty seconds after he's opened it, as determinedly and unashamedly as a surgeon closing a chest he's just sawn open after peering into its rotten insides. When he happily hands that money over every month, it's so that he can experience this terror in an infinitesimal dose, a fictional dose. What terror will move him to put his hand in his pocket now?

He receives a letter. In fact, it wakes him up (and in this detail alone there's a hint that his mother might have something to do with it), because the bell rings at eight in the morning and a very young, walleyed mailman who's even more captive to the forces of sleep than he is and who has a fresh vampire kiss on his carotid artery hands him an envelope on which he recognizes his mother's handwriting, the handwriting that his mother, unlike every other person in the world who's ever written anything by hand, has preserved unaltered, in fact it's even more beautiful and elegant than it was in her youth, when in a handful of firm, even lines that look as though they were drawn with a ruler and don't show the slightest trace of emotion or doubt she tells his father that she'll be back at the apartment on Ortega y Gasset at six p.m., and she doesn't want to find him there when she arrives, neither him nor his things. Inside the envelope is a homemade postcard produced by someone who's not very skilled at handicrafts, intended to impress more than to trick; they've stuck a photo on a piece of card and forgotten to wipe away the extra glue, which has hardened on top of the picture and now seems to be sprouting from it like cysts. It's a black-and-white photo. In that fervent way that failed artists will pounce on any existing image, especially if it's printed, to stamp their miserable human mark on it, the same clumsy hand has accentuated the shading and relief with fine, reed-like interlocking lines, so that the whole thing seems to be wrapped in a sort of wire mesh. It's a Victorian house, one of the mansions found to the north of the city, surrounded by trees and parks, which pride themselves on their longevity or ruminate on their decrepitude with arrogant indifference. It's falling to pieces, but that doesn't seem to bother his mother. Her only criticism is that you can't see the river anymore. And the mosquitoes, which swarm down in rabid gangs at night-fall and surround her—without biting her: one of the privi-leges of queens in exile—while she sits in the gallery reading the extravagant manuals she takes out of the clinic's library.

She isn't sick. She doesn't want visitors (but she wouldn't say no to cards: could he pass by the cab firm and give her new address to Mr. W.?). And no, she doesn't need money. Her lotto winnings will last her a while (although what prize wouldn't be peanuts compared with what she's lost over years of playing?). Anyway, in circumstances that don't bear recounting now but that still make her blush whenever she re-members them, the past, "a cruel tormentor, though still more generous than men," was kind enough to regurgitate into her life her psychiatrist from twenty-five years ago, a pioneer of lysergic therapies who has cancer (though even bald she's the most beautiful psychiatrist on earth) and whose last experi-ment is to assemble, or try to assemble—because not all of the candidates receive the proposal with quite the carefree de-light his mother does, putting two or three things in a bag and taking the train straight to San Isidro—the victims of the treat-ments she gave in the seventies, all brilliant, promising young things broken by acid and psychotropics, and house them for free in her clinic, indefinitely, taking advantage of the fact that her last paying patient—a deaf, almost hundred-year-old woman, the only daughter of a Central European *marchand* whose painting collection she blows on the horse races—died a few months earlier, leaving a small (20 × 25) pastel by the young Matisse among her clothes, wrapped in paper from a Viennese pastry shop. She doesn't need anything. She could swear she can't even remember what needing is. The whole world has been reduced to nothing but tasteless idiocy. Only in a sanatorium can she do the only thing she knows how to do, the only thing she wants to do, the only thing she has time for now: wait for money to rain down on her.

First his father. Now his mother. He puts the key in the lock, shoves the door with his knee—it's July, and the wood has swollen with the winter damp—and wonders whether clearing parents' apartments is his purpose, his secret calling, his true mission in the world. In fact, the trash bags he brings with him are left over from the cleaning he didn't have to do at his father's apartment. When he goes in, he doesn't know what he'll do. Sell it, throw it all away, donate it, keep some of it? He hasn't been given clear instructions. His mother's fake postcard breaks off on the threshold of the matter, just after she's asked him to take care of emptying and handing over the apartment before the end of the month, so that she doesn't have to pay another month's rent. "I'm being called," she writes, as though they were talking on the phone—a type of chiasmus that she also uses the other way around, inserting epistolary tics in the most pedestrian phone conversations—and he thinks he can hear the soft, muffled-sounding peal of an evening bell ringing to the north of the city, through the trilling of birds and the stirring of treetops in the breeze from the river, for the benefit of half a dozen survivors dressed in expensive, white, worn-out clothing, who don't know one another but who doubtless have common enemies, objects of curses and rancor, inviting them to come to dinner, or for a seven o'clock vermouth, or to play some complicated, drawn-out board game in whose dynamics lurk surprising psychological implications.

He picks up the mail that's accumulated under the door. Promotional leaflets, local pamphlets, the Auto Club magazine (addressed to the owner of the apartment), a couple of out-of-date bills, among them the unopened electricity bill with the monstrous surcharge that inspired the last of her desperate requests for money. There's nothing here that's addressed to his mother, nothing in this whole glut of paper that uses her name. Neither does anything betray her in the strict, anodyne, perfectly impersonal order that reigns here, which now that he's in his mother's space for the first time he realizes is very similar to that of short-term rentals designed entirely around middling criteria—size, layout of furniture, decoration, appliances, materials—on which nobody could ever leave their mark, even if they set their minds to it, so indifferent is everything in them to the lives that might come and inhabit them.

Why, then, does he drop the mail? He's disoriented; everything seems strange and precise, like the backdrop to a dream. There's no sign that she's been here, that much is true. But it's not the meticulous, terrible sort of emptiness that comes with cleaning after a funeral, either, which renews a space only at the price of amplifying the echo of the tragedy that took place in it. After all, his mother has always boasted about her talent for making it seem as though she was never there. And anyway, she's alive, more alive than ever in her sumptuous, damp, unheated exile, under rotting rafters that barely support the ceilings. Maybe that's exactly what's upsetting him: the idea that she's saved herself, and that, saved, she's farther from him than if she were dead. He looks around him. There's not a thing out of place. He doesn't know where to start. Instead of opening the blinds, he turns on all the lights. He doesn't want air. He wants this scene to remain just as his mother left it. Maybe he thinks that if he keeps it closed off, without any contact with the outside world, it will gradually lose its air of civilization, will heat up, ferment, and rot—with him inside. There are no messages on the answering machine: only his mother's voice feigning interest in receiving them, along with the long pauses she leaves between words as though she were talking to a foreigner or someone with learning difficulties, when in fact she's just worried that she's misunderstood the machine's instruction manual and is doing something wrong. He opens drawers more or less at random, just to feel like he's doing something, like the trip hasn't been a waste. A few sheets of blank paper, two black pencils, a couple of envelopes, a card from a local real estate company. Worse than a hotel room.

He goes into the bedroom and flops facedown on the bed. He'd like to go to sleep and dream about something extravagant and enlightening—an adventure in a castle with vertiginous stairs, ping-pong tables, tortoises fornicating or headbutting each other, and a fog that rises up and ambushes it all—then wake up not knowing where he is and gradually come back around, resting his eyes on the things around him until he recognizes them and, finally, remembers everything. The feet of the nightstand, for example, with their stylized taper, like a knock-kneed cartoon heroine's legs. The wire from the bedside lamp, which twists and runs out of view as though hiding. The painted baseboard, which has started to warp and will soon come away from the wall. A patch of gray carpet. A piece of yarn or cable tracing a red Z on the carpet. He picks it up: it's one of the fine, flexible wires coated in plastic that people use to throttle bags and containers. He turns over and lies faceup, so that a blade from the ceiling fan is pointing directly at his chest, and only then does he notice the one personal touch that's at odds with the place's neutrality: that smell. Wafting in the background is an old, dirty perfume, ancient but not overpowering: the unmistakable aroma of objects that have passed through many hands, like the smell of worn-out secondhand clothes, for example, especially when they've been shut away in a closet for a long time. Or the smell of money.

There are no worn-out clothes in his mother's closet. Or there are, but they're all impeccable, recently washed, dresses and coats fresh from the dry cleaner's and wrapped in plastic sheaths, pants ironed, shoes shining, everything hanging perfectly on the dark, wooden, slightly concave hangers that seem to be designed for shoulders and backs from another age, but which his mother is still willing to travel the length of the city to buy. The closet is full of clothes, full to bursting, so full that he wonders what could possibly have been removed, which two or three items she put in her suitcase the day she decided to admit herself to the clinic. When he looks down at the two rows of shoes covering the floor—the second on tiptoes with the heels resting against the wall to make a little more space—he sees something glinting, a sort of spark at the bottom of some low rain boots. He bends down—a raincoat caresses his head and messes up his hair as he enters a cloud of leather—and unearths a little packet of clear cellophane, like the ones that come with candy or party favors inside, tied at one end with a red wire like the one he found on the rug.

There's money inside, a few creased notes. He holds it up to his eyes with a look of surprise and suspicion, the same look people use with worrying gifts whose wrapping gives away but also contradicts their contents, the sumptuous packaging evidently having been the object of great care even though the contents are so worthless that it's difficult to even think of them as a gift, or the other way around, the wrapping an emergency measure, improvised using cheap materials, and the contents an incalculable joy. But a gift? He's not even sure that it's intended for anyone, and not simply a method of safekeeping. He pulls the closet doors wide open and lets in the light from the room, and after squatting and scanning the two rows of shoes, he finds another packet hidden in a pair of loafers, and another squashed under the sole of a sandal, and yet another being badly crushed by a pair of knee-high boots.

They're all small amounts, petty cash, and always different and very specific quantities that seem to correspond to some immediate need: twenty-five pesos, forty, thirty-two, two hundred and twenty, a hundred and ten. It's not saved cash. It's unspent cash: cash that was originally meant to pay for something, or settle something, but was stopped at the last minute and kept here, in this hothouse his mother confined it to, where she's been leading this sterile life for how long now? How long has his mother been collecting money? Those hundred and twelve pesos, for example. That's the exact amount on the electricity bill he picked up off the floor as soon as he came into the apartment, the one that prompted his mother's last request for money. It's *that* cash. Not just the same amount but the same notes he gave her: two fifties, a ten, and a two. On one of the fifties he recognizes the text from a superstitious chain his mother read aloud through laughter when she received it. He presses farther into the closet, possessed by a strange fury and willing to scour it to the last square centimeter. He finds more money, nests of it scattered between sweaters, in a drawer full of bras, hidden among socks and on the T-shirt shelf, where they're sprouting like mothball mines or Easter surprises. It's always *his* money: everything he's ever lent her, everything he's given her to spend, pay, cover, save herself from the emergencies she was drowning in. They turn up in the drawers of her nightstand, among earplugs and broken pairs of glasses; in the medicine cabinet in the bathroom, cuddling up to bottles of painkillers; in the kitchen, in the cutlery drawer and the pantry and even the oven—two little silver packets gleaming in the darkness, sitting in the middle of a baking tin like precocious stars in a black-light theater—and when he begins to open these little packets, he discovers that the money goes back in time, regresses, getting younger and older at the same time. There are notes and coins here from five, ten, twenty, forty years ago: australs, Argentine pesos, pesos ley, pesos moneda nacional, in unpredictable and at the same time strangely obtuse amounts—3,205; 22,000; 440; 27. They're like pieces of a puzzle, singular sums with irregular edges that only fit in certain holes, precise times and places at which his mother's life is bound to his. He's rolling in money now. He has more money than he's ever had before or will ever have again. But it's lost money, at once barren and glorious and as devastating as the fossils that, when they're first excavated, seem to say something so unique about the world that they're celebrated as providential discoveries for humanity, but later, when they're scrupulously, patiently examined, bring sorrow and end up dashing all hopes, because the language they say it in is dead, not impenetrable but literally dead, only ever spoken by two people, almost always without knowing they were speaking it, and often without knowing what they were saying, or why, or what special value, what sparkle, what dark privilege graced this thing they blindly mistook for common currency.

A Note on the Text

The fictional events in this novel unravel over decades of real tragedy in Argentina. It is widely known outside of the country that a military junta seized power in 1976 and went on to wage a Dirty War, "disappearing" tens of thousands of dissidents and people believed to be dissidents. That tragedy didn't occur in isolation; it was preceded by five other coups d'état in the same century, and took place amid extreme instability in all spheres, notably the economic and industrial as well as the political—though obviously distinctions like these are often academic.

Between the first summer we see here in Mar del Plata in 1966 and the conclusion of the novel around four decades later, Argentina had five currencies, whose names recur in the novel: pesos moneda nacional, pesos ley 18.188, pesos argentinos, australs, and the peso convertible—introduced in 1992 and still in use at the time of writing, though it's usually simply called the peso. Each new currency was introduced because the last had been devalued by vertiginous inflation.

For individuals, the instability of the local currency led to a reliance on the U.S. dollar that persists today. For many Argentines wishing to safeguard their cash, converting into dollars has long been a no-brainer—a reaction to economic instability that further devalues the peso.

The question of getting your hands on dollars in Argentina inevitably brings you face-to-face with the parallel—or black market—economy. The government sets an official exchange rate, but also keeps strict controls on the amount of dollars officially in circulation, sending most buyers into the black market. The rate offered at unofficial exchange outlets known as *cuevas*, or caves, is wildly more pricy than the government's official rate. And "unofficial" isn't quite the right description, either: the parallel economy is so huge and so influential in Argentina that it has its own set of rules; there's an "official" dollar exchange rate within this unofficial sector. The novel's *arbolitos* occupy a black market within the black market, offering yet another exchange rate, this one even more extortionate.

Acknowledgments

A History of Money was completed in July 2012 at the artists' retreat at Castello di Fosdinovo, beneath the protective wing of Pietro Malaspina and Maddalena Fossombroni, who make hospitality an art, and the benevolent influence of the ghost of Bianca Maria Aloisia.